REAPER'S LEGACY

TIM LEBBON

REAPER'S LEGACY

TOXIC CITY

BOOK ONE

an imprint of **Prometheus Books**
Amherst, NY

Published 2013 by Pyr®, an imprint of Prometheus Books

Cover illustration © Steve Stone
Jacket design by Nicole Sommer-Lecht

Inquiries should be addressed to
Pyr
59 John Glenn Drive
Amherst, New York 14228–2119
VOICE: 716–691–0133
FAX: 716–691–0137
WWW.PYRSF.COM

17 16 15 14 13   5 4 3 2 1

Library of Congress Cataloging-in-Publication Data

Lebbon, Tim.
    Reaper's legacy / by Tim Lebbon.
       p. cm. — (Toxic city : bk. 2)
    ISBN 978–1–61614–767–9 (cloth)
    ISBN 978–1–61614–768–6 (ebook)
    1. London (England)—Fiction. 2. Great powers—Fiction. I. Title.

PS3612.E245R43 2013
813'.6—dc23

                2012048901

Printed in the United States of America

For my own special children, Ellie and Dan

CHAPTER ONE
THE ROOKERY

B eside the tumbled wreck of the London Eye, on the banks of a River Thames clogged with refuse, the rubble of bombed buildings, and an occasional floating body, Lucy-Anne sees a woman waiting for her. The woman is dressed in normal clothing, yet possesses an ethereal quality that makes her shine. Her hair dances to an absent breeze. She moves across the pavement almost without walking, seemingly imitating one of the many mime artists who used to work this place, dressing up and painting themselves to lure coin from foreign visitors. Yet there is nothing at all fake about this woman. Against her stark reality, the backdrop of ruined London appears sketched onto the sky.

Lucy-Anne walks towards the woman, climbing over piles of twisted steel and shattered glass. She never looks away, in case the woman vanishes. *Stay there, I need to talk to you*, she thinks, because behind that idea is the certainty that this woman will tell her the truth.

And Lucy-Anne has lived in a world of lies for so long.

The woman turns to walk away, and Lucy-Anne calls after her. But though she opens her mouth she can issue no noise. Her cry is silent.

Walking along the riverbank, the woman turns and looks back. She is smiling. It's an expression that does not appear at home on her face. Even the intense flash that follows does nothing to illuminate its origins.

Lucy-Anne flinches, squeezing her eyes shut against the explosion. The ground thumps at her feet. Fallen steel groans, as if in sadness at the fresh destruction about to be wrought upon it. And way past the woman, north of London's heartland and past the false edifices of tower blocks and grand architecture, a ball of flame expands from the new wound in the land.

Firestorm scours along the river, turning water to steam, snatching old bridges from their mountings and ripping them to shreds, shattering any glass remaining in buildings and then scorching the buildings themselves.

The cloud of fire and smoke is expanding, being sucked upward into the horribly familiar mushroom cloud that Lucy-Anne had always believed was a fear from the past.

She reaches for the woman, who seems untouched by the firestorm, unconcerned at the dreadful explosion. But she is already turning away.

"No!" Lucy-Anne says, and this time her voice works. It is louder than the explosion, and for a moment she believes she can shout the detonation down. But London is falling, and burning, and being flattened to make way for whatever folly might come next.

The woman is walking away. Her clothes flap around her, unconcerned at the sun-hot flames melting the pavement at her feet and turning trees to instant charcoal. Each footstep is a *flutter* . . . *flutter* . . . *flutter* . . .

Lucy-Anne recognises the noise. She knows she should already be dead. The fallen ruin of the London Eye—ten thousand tons of steel and glass—is picked up and melted by the explosion, and the only sound of its demise is the symphony of countless wings.

Before the final blink of Lucy-Anne's dream, the woman glances back over her shoulder one more time. She looks like unfinished business.

The whisper of wings woke her, and Lucy-Anne tried to hear a message in the sound. But that was not her gift.

Rook was kneeling beside her. He looked concerned, and as she opened her eyes, the expression fell from his face, replaced with the customary casual smile. For a moment she thought she might have seen past his mask.

Rooks fluttered through the air behind him, and one large bird was perched on his shoulder, staring at her with dark, lifeless eyes.

"I'm fine," Lucy-Anne said, sitting up and looking around. Memory rushed in, drowning the dream and replacing it with a stranger reality. But just for a moment a dreg of the dream remained—the fire, the nuclear explosion, the strange woman's enigmatic smile—and she shivered. *Not everything I dream comes true*, she thought, but she could not be certain of that. Time had yet to tell.

Rook had brought her to St. Paul's Cathedral, and they had spent the night high in the dome, in a place called the Whispering Gallery. She wanted to ask why he had chosen somewhere so exposed and well-known, especially after the confrontation with the Choppers that had left so many dead. But then she had heard the effects the birds' fluttering wings had in the Gallery, and she knew. There was no silence here. Even with the birds roosting, the whole dome whispered to the sound of their wings. When he slept, Rook needed that.

"I don't like the silence," he told her, as if reading her thoughts.

"Why not?" Lucy-Anne asked. Rook's face dropped a little, and he turned away.

"It's dawn. Time to hunt."

"Hunt?"

"You chose to come with me, so you should see what it is I do."

"I came with you because you said you could help find my brother Andrew."

"I can," Rook said. "And I will. But come on." He led the way down out of the Whispering Gallery, and Lucy-Anne followed.

She hoped the others were okay. She'd watched Jack, Sparky, and Jenna fleeing the street, leaving burning helicopters, blazing buildings, and bodies behind. Leaving also Jack's father, Reaper, the leader of the Superiors, and Miller, one of the senior Choppers. She'd felt sad watching them go because she and Jack had been close—still were, she hoped. And Sparky and Jenna were her friends. But something had changed in Lucy-Anne the moment they'd entered the Toxic City. Discovering that her parents were dead had cemented that change, and as she'd fled from the hotel where she had discovered that fact, the city had seemed to open up around her. Running, crying, she had felt part of the city, not apart from it.

"Your friends haven't been caught," Rook said. They were walking through St. Paul's itself now, the huge cathedral eerily quiet but for their footsteps and the flutter of rooks' wings.

"How do you know?"

Rook did not need to answer. Two birds left his shoulders, three more landed there, spreading their huge wings to balance and breaking the silence with their cries.

He communes with the birds, Lucy-Anne thought. The idea was crazy, yet she accepted it completely. There was so much crazy stuff going on, including within her.

Those dreams she'd had. Dogs attacking, and then the pack of dogs had assaulted them in the tunnels into London. Her family buried, and then she'd learned that her parents were dead, and likely buried in one of London's massive mass graves. And Rook and the birds. She had dreamt of them as well, and now here they were.

"We need to go north," she said as they emerged onto the cathedral's wide steps. *Your brother is alive north of here*, the man who'd confirmed that her parents were dead had told her. The street before them was silent and still. Nothing moved.

"And we will," Rook said. He was a small, slight boy, with a dark mop of hair and almost-feminine features. But Lucy-Anne had seen him use his birds to kill.

"Andrew is all I have left," she whispered.

"No he isn't." Rook shook his head, reaching out to touch her hand. Was that affection? Ownership? She didn't know, and she flinched away. He'd said he could help her, but that didn't mean she owed him anything. Not yet.

Rook laughed softly. "Come on. East of here, there are four of them. I'll show you what I can do."

"Four of what?" He started down the steps at a jog, without answering. "Rook? Show me what?" Still he didn't answer.

At risk of losing him to the deserted, dead streets of London, Lucy-Anne followed.

There were four, as Rook had said. But one did not belong.

"What are they doing to him?"

Rook reached out quickly and pressed his hand across Lucy-Anne's mouth, then came in close so he could whisper in her ear.

"Not a word."

They were in the third floor of a once-exclusive apartment complex, looking out through net curtain at the wide street below. The trees and bushes down there, untrimmed and unchecked since Doomsday, had gone wild. Expensive cars sat on flat tyres along the centre of the street. And parked on the opposite side of the road, a dark blue Land Rover. She could just make out the driver sitting inside keeping the engine running, and outside stood two heavily-armed Choppers, and the man.

Rook's retinue of birds remained out of view. Lucy-Anne saw a few pigeons and, high overhead, a family of buzzards circled.

She watched Rook watching them, and wondered what he was here to do. Was he a spy for Reaper, gathering as much information as he could about the Choppers and what they were doing? Or was this something else?

Shouting. She returned her attention to the street, just as one of the Choppers shoved the man forward. He was crying and shivering. He looked very thin. Lucy-Anne wanted to reach out to help him, but knew she could not.

Rook had slipped his hand beneath the net curtain and flipped a catch, and Lucy-Anne held her breath as he eased the window open.

"Get on with it!" she heard the Chopper shout. "It's your last chance, you stupid bastard. You know what you've got to do, so do it!"

The other Chopper said something Lucy-Anne didn't catch, but the loud one shouted him down.

"You saw what he did to me in the back of the Rover. Just look! Bit me!" He held out his gloved hand, displaying nothing. He nursed his rifle in his other hand, barrel never wavering far from the snivelling man.

The man faced away from the Choppers, and that's how Lucy-Anne knew he was not feigning the tears. She couldn't remember the last time she'd seen anyone looking so wretched.

"Go on! Do it! *Do* it!"

The man squeezed his eyes closed and seemed to gather himself, and for a moment silence descended across the street. Lucy-Anne held her breath in anticipation of what she was about to see. *What can he do?* she thought. But nothing happened, and the man slumped down to his knees and started crying again.

"Right, well, another waste of bloody time," the Chopper said. "Got the camera ready?" His colleague chuckled and nodded as the soldier raised his rifle, sighting on the back of the man's head.

Rook glanced sidelong at Lucy-Anne, eyes glittering, as if testing her.

She screamed, "Leave him alone!"

Rook chuckled, then grabbed her arm and pulled her back from the window.

Machine-gun fire raked the building's façade, shattering windows, bullets ricocheting, the sound unbelievable where it was channeled back and forth between the high buildings. Lucy-Anne curled into a ball and watched bullets stitching the plaster ceiling above her.

Rook was crawling towards the back of the room, and as he knelt up he whistled, a high-pitched sound which seemed so unnatural coming from a human mouth. He seemed suddenly more alive than she had seen him before, and for a moment as he raised his arms she thought he might take flight, mimicking the birds he seemed so close to, and over which he exerted such control.

The gunfire halted.

"The man!" Lucy-Anne said, but Rook was only grinning. He whistled again, attracting another burst of gunfire. They were shooting blind. The Choppers had no idea who was watching them, or from where.

The light from outside suddenly faded, and even beneath the staccato gunfire she could hear the descent of birds.

Rook laughed out loud, revelling in what he was doing. "Come and see!" he said, grabbing Lucy-Anne's hand and pulling her to the window on her knees. Broken glass cut their legs, but neither of them took any notice. The scene outside was so amazing that it eased away the pain.

Rooks filled the street, shadowing her view of anything beyond the window, fragmenting it so that she only caught brief, fleeting glimpses of what was happening—the Choppers shooting, their hands waving, the guns dropped, arms flapping, bodies falling beneath the onslaught of birds. The Land Rover started reversing along the street, engine protesting, and then it impacted a BMW that had not moved in two years. Its windows starred, then broke. Its insides turned black, and then red.

"What about him?" she said, leaning left and right as she tried to spot the man the Choppers had brought here for whatever reason. "Where is he? Rook?" She glanced at Rook, then back down to the street.

"He needs to keep still," Rook said. He was concentrating. "Sometimes the birds . . ." He shrugged, unconcerned.

"You're as bad as Reaper," she said.

"I'm nothing like Reaper," Rook said. "I'm on my own. Come on. There'll be more arriving soon."

"But . . ." The noise outside was already decreasing, and the air seemed to be thinning and growing lighter as the rooks spiralled up and out of view over the rooftops. Left behind, evidence of the terrible deaths they had brought down with them, at the behest of the young man in whose hands she had placed herself. The two Choppers were tattered remnants of humanity. The Land Rover's engine had died, windscreen splashed red from the inside. And as she watched, the terrified Irregular slowly raised his head and looked around, struggled to his feet, and hobbled away down the street.

We should help him, she thought. He was trailing blood. Perhaps a Chopper had got a lucky shot off before the birds descended. But even as she had the thought, she realised that he would slow them down. He would be an encumbrance, and Rook was right—more Choppers would soon arrive.

"We've really gotta go," Rook said.

Lucy-Anne looked back at the slaughtered Choppers. One of them was scratching slowly at the rough road surface, but his eyes stared sightless into the gutter. Last breaths. "I'm staying here."

"Fair enough." He left the room, and the sudden stillness and silence were startling. Lucy-Anne held her breath.

It was thirty seconds before Rook reappeared, his smile tensed with frustration.

"I'll come if you tell me why you've got so much hate," she said. "You smile, but . . ."

"Yeah," Rook said, looking down at his feet. It was the first time he'd allowed her to see him sad. She supposed it was a start.

They were walking along a narrow pathway between high-walled gardens, pushing through rose and clematis bushes that had run rampant in the two years since Doomsday. It surprised Lucy-Anne just how much things had grown in such a short time, almost as if nature had been waiting for humanity to lose its grip and was revelling in newfound freedom.

Rook had not spoken for half an hour. The silence suited her, but it also made her memories of the deaths she had witnessed more vivid. There was such coldness in the boy that she could almost feel it emanating from him in waves. He made the hairs on her arms stand on end.

Each time she blinked she saw the dying Chopper scratching at the road, and wondered what last thought had been going through his or her mind.

Lucy-Anne maintained the silence, hoping that he would start telling her about himself without prompting. But every moment that passed increased the pressure of the quietness between them, until it became so great that she thought the air might break.

"Tell me why all the hate," she said at last.

Rook stopped and turned, pushing her back against a wall. For a moment she thought he was going to attack her, and she was aware of his birds shadowing the air around them, like black bags carried on the breeze. His eyes glimmered dark. His lips were pressed tight, pale. But then he sighed, relaxed his grip on her throat, and stepped back. His fingers lingered against her skin, a silent apology.

"I hate them because they killed my brother." He was looking at her shoulder, unable to meet her eyes. "They dragged him away soon after Doomsday, cut him up . . ." He waved away whatever images the recollection invoked.

"Go on," Lucy-Anne said. Rook veered from anger to confusion, not used to exposing himself so much. But then he seemed to settle and started speaking.

"David. He was my twin but so much more . . . special. He could speak to the birds. All of them, from the smallest wren to the biggest buzzard. They'd drift down and perch so close to him that he could touch them. It was amazing, and he kept it from everyone but me."

"Why keep it from people?" she asked, confused. Wasn't everyone in London special nowadays?

"Because he was like that when we were little kids together, then older kids, then all through our teens. And it was only after Doomsday that it troubled him enough to get caught."

She frowned, confused.

"He was like you," Rook said. "Special all on his own, before all this."

"Like me?"

"I dreamed of you because you dreamed of me," Rook said softly, and it was the most emotion she'd heard him convey. He was opening himself to her, and at the same time his doubt about doing so was obvious. He'd been closed up tight for so long that this was hurting.

"I *did* dream of you," she whispered.

"And that's why I want to help you," Rook said. "Because you're like David. Pure. Don't you see? You weren't even here when it happened, and still you're *so special*. Not like me. Changed into this by Doomsday and all the shit that's come after." He turned suddenly and walked away. Overhead, rooks followed them, flitting from roof to roof, all of them totally silent.

Lucy-Anne ran after him. She could not shake from her mind's eye the image from her dream—that strange woman on the banks of the Thames, and the nuclear explosion that had seemed to pass her by.

"They're just dreams! They can't *all* come true."

"I came true," Rook said over his shoulder. He continued walking away, and Lucy-Anne could only follow.

CHAPTER TWO
MAJESTY

Jack stared along the barren wilderness of the Mall towards Buckingham Palace and wondered what had become of the Queen. Had she died at her first inhalation of Evolve, just like so many of her subjects? Or was she now someone with incredible, almost supernatural powers, a human being rapidly evolving into something greater—a fire starter, a healer, someone capable of impossible things?

As far as Jack was aware, no one had seen the Queen since Doomsday. Perhaps on his quest he would meet her, and her majesty would be revealed.

"Stop arsing about!" Sparky hissed. He was Jack's best friend, heavily built with spiked blond hair, and a lighthearted manner that hid darker depths. "Jenna's gonna be waiting."

"Yeah," Jack said. He closed his eyes briefly, and for a while he was his old self. He was glad. He felt so much closer to his friends like this.

All through the previous night, following his confrontation with his father and their escape from the scene of so much death and destruction, Jack had been sensing a change happening inside. The Nomad's touch was working through him at its own strange pace. He was infected, but he had an idea that his own burgeoning powers were something different from his father's, or Rosemary's . . . or perhaps anyone else in London right now.

He had hidden himself, Sparky, and Jenna away from view in a basement while a Chopper looked right at them, and made the soldier not see. And he didn't know for sure how he had done so. *Invis-*

ible! Jenna had gasped, but Sparky had been more wary, eyeing his friend as he considered what had happened.

Jack was still not sure whether he had influenced their presence, or the Chopper's ability to see them.

Sparky grabbed his arm. "We need to get across Trafalgar Square sharpish! Don't like it here, it's too open. Anyone could be watching."

"We'll be okay," Jack said.

Sparky frowned at him.

"No special powers," Jack said. "Just a feeling. Come on, let's find Jenna."

They ran up from the end of the Mall towards the square, crossing streets once crammed nose to tail with vehicles. Now it was jammed with a motionless traffic jam that might never move again. Many cars had their doors closed and windows obscured by a pale green growth inside, and Jack had no wish to see what might be hidden.

The square was home to thousands of pigeons, and the birds took flight in sweeping waves as Jack and Sparky ran across. That was a good sign as far as Jack was concerned; it meant that no one else was around to startle the birds aloft. *Unless they're like that boy Lucy-Anne's gone off with*, he thought. Sadness stabbed at the loss of his old girlfriend.

They skirted around one of the huge plinths bearing a proud, gigantic lion, and Jack looked up past it at Admiral Nelson on top of his column. Nelson's view of London must be a sad one.

"There," Sparky said, pointing. Jack followed his friend, trying not to see the mass of clothing and other things that filled one of the fountains. People had used to come here on New Year's Eve to drink and celebrate and dance one year into the next, filled with hope for what the future might bring.

They met Jenna in front of the National Gallery, crouched down behind a pile of split black plastic bags spilling mouldy clothes. Sparky and Jenna touched hands briefly—they had progressed from good friends to lovers only recently, and their vitality was evident —and she looked at Jack with wide eyes.

"I've made contact," she said. "They're bringing him to a meeting point now, and he'll check us over. But . . ."

"But what?" Jack prompted.

"They say he's dying."

"Well, if he can't help us we're lost," Sparky said. He glanced back at Jack, as if expecting him to dispute his statement.

But Jack couldn't. Miller and the Choppers were searching for them now—Miller knew that Jack had been touched by the mysterious Nomad, and his greatest desire now to was get hold of Jack and examine him. Dissect him, perhaps. See what was going on inside.

And what was? Jack wasn't sure.

"Guys, I'm feeling pretty lost anyway," Jack said. "You both know something's happening with me, but I don't really know what. Different things . . . and not all the time. I can't . . ." He looked around, waved across the square. "I can't topple Nelson's Column with my mind, or see around corners. Or change this pile of clothes into stone. Or . . ." He shrugged, voice breaking, throat filling. He spoke quieter. "Maybe I'll be able to do all those things tomorrow. But today, the only thing stopping me going mad with this is you two. My mates."

Jenna smiled at him, eyes glittering.

"Pussy," Sparky said.

Jack laughed softly. "Yeah. So come on. Let's see if this old guy can help."

From the moment he saw the old man, Jack knew that he was dying from something unknown. It was the same malady killing the Irregulars in the underground hospital where he'd found his mother. An incredible man—Jack hoped he could still use his gift—he was suffering from the mysterious illness affecting more and more of London's survivors.

He was mad, first of all. Sitting in an old shopping trolley in the shattered entrance to a once-posh store, scrunched up like a skinny rag doll, the man seemed to be snatching at unseen flies bothering him. He stared, motionless, and then a hand would lash out, fist closing on nothing.

"What's he doing?" Sparky asked.

"Don't know," Jenna said. "Same when I found him. I thought he was eating flies, but I don't think there's anything there."

"Just cos you don't see nothing, don't mean there's nothing there." The man glared at them, his wide white eyes startling, dreadlocks gathered across his shoulders, chest, and drawn up knees like a hundred twisting snakes. Although sitting in the trolley, he seemed animated with constant movement.

Deeper in the ruined store, Jack could see the shadows of other people observing them. The glint of light on metal—a gun? Something about that comforted him. These weird powers were troubling, and beside them a gun was almost mundane.

They'd been told that this man would be able to tell whether they were being followed or spied upon, and whether the Choppers could trace them. Jack had found the tracking chip in the photo of his mother, but perhaps there was something more.

"So can you do it?" he asked.

"Kids," the man said. His age was ambiguous; he could have been forty or sixty. "Just not polite anymore."

"Can you do it, *please?*" Sparky said.

The man's hand snapped out, arm surprisingly long, and he clenched his hand close to Sparky's face. Drew it in close to his nose, eyes rolling slightly, trolley wheels squeaking with movement. His dreadlocks shimmered and squirmed, and his shoulders shook. He inhaled and closed his eyes.

"You're all right," he said.

"Good," Jack said. "Thanks. So now—"

"Didn't say you," the man said. "You, you got more about you." He wasn't quite staring at Jack. All around him, but not *quite* at him. "Doubts, and hidden things. Weird."

"Yeah," Jack said. "Tell me about it."

The man turned suddenly and reached for Jenna, stretching out from the trolley and almost tipping it over. She flinched back, but his fist closed and plucked several dark hairs from her head. He drew them quickly to his face and breathed in. Wheels squeaked.

"Shit," Sparky said, glancing at Jack. "We could've just run."

"We've been running all night," Jack said.

"You're fine," the man said to Jenna. He turned back to Jack, letting Jenna's plucked hair go to float down around him. "Now, back to you. To you. You."

"What do you need?" Jack asked.

The man was frowning. His eyes grew wider, and he started keening, crunching up in pain.

Someone emerged from the shadowy shop. The short woman glanced at Jack and his friends, and Jack saw a look in her eyes that he recognised from his mother. She had been made some sort of a healer by the effects of Doomsday, but she was someone who had always cared.

"He's very sick," the woman said. "You should leave him now."

"I can't," Jack said. "He hasn't checked me yet. I need to know if I'm being watched."

"He's weak and needs rest," the woman said. She sounded so weary and sad.

"Is it the same as the others?" Jack asked.

The woman looked at him in surprise. "You're outsiders. You've seen others suffering from this?"

"My mother worked in a hospital under Stockwell tube station," he said.

The woman sighed, nodded. "The same. It affects the mind, and the body, and withers them both. So sad. Such a loss."

"Especially with the powers they all have," Jenna said.

"No," the woman said. "It's such a loss because they're people, and I can't do a thing to help."

"You're watched," the man said. His voice was incredibly low, almost vibrating through the ground. Even the carer stepped back. "You're known. You're . . . observed . . . by . . . *her*."

By Nomad, Jack thought, but he did not speak her name.

"Take him away," Jack said. But the man had stopped shaking and was looking at Jack now, one long, thin arm raised, fingers clawed as if to tear something out of the air.

"She's waiting to see," he rumbled. Pigeons took flight at his voice, and Jack felt the words resounding in his chest, his belly. "See if the . . . seed . . . took . . ." He sighed and slumped down, muttering something as his hair closed across his face as if to hide him from view.

"What was that all about?" Jenna asked. She came close to Jack, Sparky standing behind her.

"Maybe he meant Nomad," Jack whispered.

"Right," Sparky said. "Great. So now what do we—"

A whistle, a whisper, a piercing pain in Jack's neck. As his vision quickly clouded he saw more shapes emerging from the shop and coming towards him. His friends fell. And he fell too, watched all the way by a presence inside that was so very far from human.

And so he sleeps. The gravity of his future draws him onward, and it frightens him. But that's fine. It should *frighten him, for a time. But soon it will entrance him as well.*

Nomad moved from one street to the next, casting her senses about now that Jack was asleep. If danger rose she would go to him, but not unless it was extreme, and not unless he could do nothing to counter it himself. He had to learn, and she was afraid of steering him the wrong way.

Afraid of encouraging in him the same madness that had taken her.

But I was different. I am the first vector, and I was there at the beginning. Evolve was so much stronger then, so much a concentrated mass of change. Confused, like an infant unsure of its abilities and potentials. Now, I am sure. I've been practising.

From where she rested, she saw.

In Peckham, a man smashed his way into a locked house and rifled through a dead family's photograph album. He cried, even though he did not know them. Nomad felt his sadness and cried with him, and the man's head snapped around as he heard the sound of a weeping woman.

In Soho, three women used their combined powers to stalk a deer. There were only seventeen wild deer left in London—Nomad knew every one of them, and could place them all given the time and peace to concentrate. But she could not deny these women the fresh meat they craved. They were all pregnant, and their children would be important. Nomad knew that, and she tried to tell the embryos so. The women paused and gasped as their children kicked against the unfairness of things, and the mothers all felt a brief, intense moment of wretchedness.

The deer escaped.

She tasted blood on the air, and traced it back to a pub in the East End. An empty bottle of whiskey, a smoking cigarette, the taste of hopelessness on the air and the tang of sharpened steel, a knife on the floor, a man bleeding his last. Another precious one gone, and Nomad's fresh tears matched his own.

Deep underground, a group of people were trying to make a home.

Seven miles to the north, a spirit haunted a deserted tower, and wondered why it was there.

Nomad moved on, passing through the toxic city she had brought into being. Every now and then she paused to lean against a wall. Inside her, something else was growing. This sickness was the only thing she could not touch or smell, see or know.

It was a mystery to her, and Nomad was no longer used to mysteries.

Jack thought perhaps they had blinded him. *There were Choppers in the shop!* But that did not make sense. The people in the shop had been Irregulars, their rendezvous had been arranged, and now he was bound and sightless, yet moving.

They were carrying him on some sort of stretcher. He struggled against his binds, but his hands and legs were tied tight. He blinked and felt no pain, yet he still couldn't see.

His memories swam, perception awash.

I'm special now, he thought, and he searched for some way to probe outward, see what was happening and try to stop it. He found nothing. For now he was just a normal boy who felt like he was going to puke.

Deep inside had been that presence, and he searched cautiously for it again. It was gone. It had left behind the scent and the sense of Nomad, and at that thought Jack realised that a hood covered his head, and he was not blind at all.

He tried to speak, but something had been taped over his mouth.

He heard voices. The stretcher was put down, and then someone spoke very close to his right ear.

"Don't be afraid, Jack." It was barely a whisper, androgynous. "We're going up, and you and your friends will be safe. There will be fear. You'll be *scared*. But trust me, there's no danger."

With a jolt they started carrying him again, and Jack prepared himself. When Rosemary had taken them down into the subterranean hospital to find his mother, a pair of twins had guarded the place, manifesting terrors in the minds of anyone who approached as a defence against the hospital being discovered. Jack had seen huge scorpions, Emily had seen moths, and Sparky for some reason had imagined giant, deadly chickens.

But the sense of fear that settled quickly over him now was terrible and all-consuming. He would have cried out, had his mouth not been bound. He writhed, then froze. His heart hammered. Everything he couldn't see was going to eat him, everything he couldn't feel or hear would crush him, consume him. The anticipation of this was more terrible than the act itself might be, and he moaned so hard against his gag that he thought his brain would erupt.

"It's safe, it's safe," that calming voice whispered, but the darkness pressed into Jack, trying to drown and crush him down.

It's safe, it's safe, he told himself. He sought something extra—a new sense, a burgeoning power—but he was simply Jack. Scared, lonely, worrying about his mother and sister held in the Choppers' Camp H, fearful of his father, the dreadful Reaper. Scared little Jack. He started to cry, wishing his mother were there to hold and calm him as she had been for most, but not all of his years.

I've only just found her, I can't lose her again!

"We're there," the voice said, and the hood was removed from Jack's head, his limbs unbound, and tape was ripped from across his mouth.

His vision swam from the tears, and he squinted his eyes against the glaring light.

"Oh, sorry." The light levels lowered. A man was revealed before Jack, silhouetted against the strip lights in the ceiling. He was tall and thin with a wild head of hair haloing his face, but his expression was in shadow.

"Who are you?" Jack asked. He gathered his composure, grabbing onto the normality of what he saw after the terrors he'd been experiencing. "Why are you doing this to us?"

"Because I have to. And my name's Breezer."

"Oh. Right. So what's your special power?"

The man chuckled and moved to the edge of the room, leaning against the wall. Across the room Sparky and Jenna sat up as they were released, and Jack locked gazes with them. Sparky looked angry, but Jack knew that they were safe. There was no threat here.

"No, that's really my name," the man said. "Bill Breezer. I'm fifty-four. I'm a heating engineer. Or used to be." He glanced at all of them, and Jack thought perhaps his smile was always there. He looked like someone who smiled a lot. Which meant that he was difficult to read.

"Where are we?" Sparky asked. The people who carried them had retreated from the large room, though Jack saw two of them just outside the open door. The room itself was sparse—bare plasterboard walls, a polished floor with holes where something had once been bolted down. A few paler patches on the walls where frames had once hung. It had the air of somewhere abandoned.

"If I felt comfortable telling you that, we wouldn't have knocked you out to bring you here."

"Thanks for this anyway," Jack said. "The Choppers almost caught us three times, at least. We can't run forever."

"No," Breezer said. "And Miller really wants you, it seems. Because . . ." His smile dropped slightly and he took on a faraway look, staring through Jack rather than at him. "Ahh. Wow. Nomad touched you."

"So you read minds," Jack said.

"I see histories. It doesn't amount to the same thing, but it can be more useful. You could have denied Nomad's touch, but I would have still known."

"You see through lies," Jenna said.

Breezer nodded. "You're all welcome here, of course. Even you, Jack."

"*Even* me?"

"Your father's a monster."

Jack bristled for a moment, but then remembered what his father had done in that suburban London street—the men and women he had killed, brutally, in cold blood. And he could hardly deny Breezer's assessment.

"He's no longer the father I knew," Jack said.

Breezer did not answer. He looked at all three of them again. Then he inclined his head and said, "So, let's eat. I'll bet you're hungry?"

Sparky nodded.

"Ahh," Breezer said. "A fan of a decent burger, Sparky?"

Sparky smiled.

"Good. Follow me. And while we're eating, we can talk about what might happen next."

They emerged into a brightly lit corridor. At the end of the corridor stood a floor-to-ceiling window offering a view out over London. The window was not far away, and Jack suffered a moment of dizziness when he realised how high they were. In the distance he could see the green chaos of a large overgrown park, and closer by stood the unmistakable silhouette of Nelson's column.

"I was sure you'd taken us underground!" Jenna said.

"We're in Heron Tower," Breezer said. "The Choppers treat us like rats, and that's their greatest mistake. Here, we can hide in plain sight. And just in case we're compromised, there are various escape routes below and above."

"Above?" Jack asked.

Sparky stepped towards the window.

"Don't!" Breezer said. "We try to stay away. Don't want to risk casting shadows."

"Right," Sparky said. He looked for a moment longer, then turned around. "You mentioned burgers?"

Jack's query unanswered, Breezer walked back along the corridor, and Jack and his friends followed.

They entered a large former office area. The desks were now pushed against one wall, and dividing screens had been ranked a few feet from the panoramic windows. Plants in large square pots had long ago withered and died, brittle sculptures to a forgotten past. The windows themselves were dusty, filtering sunlight and blurring the views beyond.

There were still some touches that saddened Jack, office workers' attempts to personalise their space—kids' drawings stuck to some of the regular concrete columns, photographs of drunken office outings, and on one desk a collection of old, stained mugs. Whatever purpose this office had served seemed pointless now.

There were several Irregulars in the large open-plan area. Most of them sat in swivel chairs reading or staring from the windows, and two were hunkered over an enclosed metal gas barbecue. Heavenly smells were issuing from there, and Jack's mouth started to water.

"Right then," Sparky said, and he walked on ahead of them.

Jenna surprised Jack by taking his hand. "We'll be all right," she said. "All of us."

"I wish you could see the future," Jack said, smiling at his friend. She smiled back and kissed him on the cheek.

They gathered around the barbecue, and Jack was surprised to see no flames, and smell no gas. There was not even a gas bottle in sight. Then he saw that one of the Irregulars had her hand pressed to the metal container's underside, and she was frowning in concentration.

"Medium rare, please," Sparky said, grinning at Jack and Jenna. Jack laughed out loud, and it was a release of tension that felt so good he did it again. Jenna laughed too. Breezer smiled uncertainly.

The barbecue was opened and food served onto scratched china plates. The several Irregulars melted away then, leaving Breezer alone with them. They ate in silence for a few minutes, and Jack could not help smiling. Such a surreal scene. London bathed in summer sun beyond the windows, so distant that it might have been back to normal. And they were eating human-heated burgers in an office block.

"Delicious!" Sparky said through a full mouth. Grease dribbled down his chin and caught in his fuzzy stubble. "Best beefburger I've tasted in ages."

"Thank you," Breezer said. "We do what we can." He took a delicate bite of his own meal and chewed for a few moments. "It's not beef."

All movement froze. Jack looked from Sparky, to Jenna, to Breezer. Then Sparky shrugged and took another huge bite, making appreciative noises with each munch.

"What are you doing here?" Jack said. "You seem to be in charge, and—"

Breezer's high laugh surprised them all. "I'm not in charge!" he said. "Jack. You make us sound like Superiors."

"Well . . ." Jack nodded after the people who had left the large room.

"We're surviving," Breezer said. "Doing our very best, that's all. There's not much trust about these days, so when a few people find others they *can* trust, they tend to stay together." He looked at his food, no longer seeming hungry. "It's not quite family. But as close as we have."

"You have family outside London?" Jenna asked.

"Wife," Breezer said. "My two sons. I lost some more distant relatives on Doomsday, but not my close family. They're out there somewhere. Think I'm dead."

"And haven't you ever wanted to try to get out to them?" Jenna asked.

"Of course! In the beginning escape was all any survivor wanted. But the government quickly threw a cordon around London, and the Choppers blasted whole districts to rubble so that—"

"Yeah, we saw that," Jack said.

"Right. Well, there was so much confusion. The huge numbers of dead started to decompose, stinking the city up. There was disease, and carrion creatures—dogs, cats, rats. *Lots* of rats. Everyone was grieving for someone, everyone was confused and scared. No one knew what the hell had happened, and why the authorities weren't trying to help. There were a lot of suicides. And on top of all that, we started to feel . . . different."

"The powers," Jenna said.

"It drove a lot of people close to madness. Some still are, and you'd do best to avoid those. But a lot of people tried to escape, yes. Overground, underground, covertly, aggressively. A few even tried air balloons. They were all caught and executed. Sometimes the Choppers left their bodies on display. Once, fifteen corpses rotted on lamp posts in Oxford Street. That was Christmas of the first year." Breezer trailed off as he remembered terrible things.

"But you could burst out, couldn't you?" Sparky asked. "Combine, use powers to find a weak spot, an escape route like Rosemary did. Get out and spread the word about the deception."

"They'd know," Breezer said.

"But we came in through tunnels," Jack said. "Five of us and Rosemary snuck in."

"Six of you?" Breezer said, nodding. "Yeah, it's possible they knew that, too."

"But how?" Jenna asked.

Breezer glanced from one to the other of them, as if waiting for something.

"'Cos they've got one working for him," Sparky said. The blond boy was staring at the open barbecue and the spare burgers steaming there, but he no longer looked hungry. He looked furious.

"No," Jack said, shaking his head. "No! With everything they've done? All the people they've captured and *chopped up?*"

"It's not for sure," Breezer said. "A rumour that has only just surfaced. But it's said there was a child in the beginning who could feel the *weight* of people moving around London. Don't ask me how. How can I tell your truth from your lies? But if she was in Kensington, she could tell if a group of people were walking across Piccadilly Circus. She called it following the city's pulse, so it's said. And three months after Doomsday, the Choppers took her."

"But they didn't kill her," Sparky said.

"Why doesn't she find you lot?" Jenna asked.

"We live here together, but are careful only to gather in threes or fours. And it's said she only tracks moving people, not those just . . ."

"Just living somewhere," Jack finished for him.

"Bloody hell," Sparky said.

"Yeah." Jack was nodding slowly.

"So if you form an army . . ." Jenna began, but she did not need to finish.

"And now even that option is being taken away," Jack said, and he stared Breezer in the eye. "Because you're all dying."

Breezer nodded, turning grim. "You saw Milton down in the street. Until a few weeks ago he was as strong as you or me, and now . . . well, he's mad, and fading fast. None of us knows what the illness is, where and when it will manifest. No healer can touch it. It's a mystery."

"Do the Superiors suffer from it as well?"

"I don't know," Breezer said. "There are so few of them, and they have little contact with us. Sometimes I think they view us as low as the Choppers."

"But you have an idea of what it is," Jenna said, a statement more than a question. Jack smiled secretly. She'd always been good at steering conversations.

"I've been studying it," Breezer admitted. "Questioning as many Irregulars as I can."

"Seeing through lies," Jenna said.

"Finding the truth."

"Which is?" Jack asked.

"Well, you know the basics. Evolve killed most of those it touched, and those who survived quickly developed a range of powers and abilities. Almost all of them were psychological. Some . . . almost supernatural. That's Evolve's first mystery. What I do think is that whether a person now calls themselves Irregular or Superior depends upon how dramatic the power they're developed. Superiors tend to have destructive, or more physically powerful abilities. Less human, some might say. The far more numerous Irregulars are healers, truth-seers, way finders. Other things, too."

"I'd figured that one out myself," Jack said, thinking of what his father had become—Reaper, a man who killed with his voice—and those accompanying him. "The woman who brought us into London wanted the Irregulars and the Superiors to unite. Force their way out, and expose themselves to the world."

"I know Rosemary well," Breezer said, nodding slowly.

"You don't agree with her?" Jenna asked.

"On the contrary, I was one of those who suggested the possibility in the first place. And I knew who she was creeping out of London to find. I'm convinced the only way anyone will leave

London alive is if the Superiors join with the rest of us. It was a long, long shot, thinking that bringing Reaper's children in would change the way he is. Persuade him to cooperate. But now . . ." Breezer looked at Jack with hungry eyes, and Jack glanced away to Jenna and Sparky. They were tensed, more alert. Worried. They all sensed a change in the conversation.

"Now what?" Sparky asked.

"Now that *you're* changing, Jack, maybe you'll be the one to lead us out. And I truly believe that the only hope of curing what's slowly killing us is to appeal to people outside. There are amazing people in London, but we need doctors and scientists, not diviners and fire starters."

"You need normal people," Jenna said.

"Yes," Breezer said. "The world has to know the truth, because we need their help."

"Then our plan stands," Jack said. "Escape London, expose the lie that everyone outside has been told. Reveal the truth."

"Tell everyone that London isn't just inhabited by monsters," Sparky said.

"Well, mostly," Jenna said.

"We'll help you in any way we can," Breezer said. "But the sickness is spreading, and more and more people are succumbing. Everything's against the clock now, Jack."

"Not without my mother," Jack whispered. "And not without my sister."

"But *you* can lead us! No one has ever been touched by Nomad. Few people have even seen her, and most still consider her a myth! Your powers might be—"

Jack slammed his hand on the table. Cups jumped and spilled water, a plate shook to the floor and shattered. The impact echoed around the office, a haunting sound that slowly faded before anyone spoke.

"I didn't come to start a war," Jack said. "I'm no leader, and whatever's happening to me . . ." He was both angry and scared, so he concentrated on something solid that he felt could hold him firm—love. "I'm going for my mother and sister. They're what matters to me. And perhaps at the same time we can stop the girl. Blind the Choppers. Then you won't need *anyone* to lead you out."

"But no one knows where Camp H is," Breezer said. "And even if you did, there's no way—"

"There *is* a way." Jack thought of Reaper, and the sense of fatherhood he'd sensed still within him. He had shunned Jack and sent him away to be hunted by Choppers, and yet Jack would as much give up on his father as he would his mother and sister, Emily.

He stood, and his friends stood with him. "We need to rest," Jack said. Breezer nodded. But the air had chilled, and the silence that accompanied them back to their room was loaded.

"Are you *crazy?*" Jenna said. "He abandoned you, Jack. Sent you and us away, a ten-minute head start before he let the Choppers come after us again. He doesn't give a shit about you or us. And you want to go out there and find him again?"

Jack nodded.

"Maybe he'll just kill us next time," Jenna said. "And do you think he'll be that easy to find?" She was standing by the closed door to the small office. Jack leaned in the corner, and Sparky had taken the only seat, plate balanced on his lap with the remains of another burger cooling on it.

"I think I can find him, yes," Jack said. He breathed deeply, trying to open himself up and not fear anymore. And with the memory of Nomad's finger on his tongue came a rush of startling sensations. Seeds of potential sparked in his mind like stars being born to an empty universe. He let them shine, and chose one.

The ability was shocking and felt unreal, not his to own. And yet one look at Sparky set his friend sweating, gasping for air and loosening his collar. Sweat dribbled down his forehead and cheeks, and as his eyes drooped Jack pulled back, not wishing to make his friend faint.

Sparky spilled his burger to the floor. "That was you?"

"Yeah." Jack closed his eyes and glimpsed his expanding universe. It was utterly terrifying, and exhilarating. Nomad's touch had been the big bang, and now his inner perception was shatteringly huge, filled with swirling clouds of light coalescing into points of potential. He could move in the blink of an eye, and from one moment to the next he would be orbiting one power, or another. He knew them, and knowing scared him. This was so new. Still chaotic. Dangerous.

"Well, I'm with Jack," Sparky said.

Jenna looked frightened, uncertain.

"Don't be scared," Jack said, moving towards her.

"I'm not," she said, but she waved her hands at him, urging him back. "Well, I am, I *am* scared. But we're together. That's it, I suppose. We're together, and nothing comes between us. So if you think you can find him and get him to help, that's what we do."

"Yeah!" Sparky said. "Friends forever! We should cut our thumbs and be blood brothers. And sister."

"Oh, Sparky," Jenna said, shaking her head.

They just smiled at each other instead.

CHAPTER THREE
THE FALL

I see a woman laughing in the face of a mushroom cloud. Lucy-Anne wished she could say this to Rook, and make him understand her confusion and desperation. But it was only a dream. And surely not *all* dreams could come true.

Besides, it was thoughts of her brother that drove her. With her parents dead, and likely buried in those mass burial pits that she and the others had walked across only days ago (and *that* was something she'd dreamed as well), he was all she had left.

Andrew. Five years older than her, he'd always been the sensible one, the apple of her mother's eye even though Lucy-Anne knew that her father had a soft spot for her own mild rebellious streak. When Andrew was revising for his exams, Lucy-Anne would be out with her friends, choosing makeup her mother never liked her wearing and clothes that were really too adult for a thirteen-year-old. He played football for his school. She played hooky *from* school. Deep down he'd made her jealous, and she'd annoyed the hell out of him. But she'd never loved him as much as she did now that he was gone.

Rook had taken them down to the river, and now they were working their way west. He'd told her there were easier routes north from that direction. The Thames was sluggish and thick as gravy, and Lucy-Anne tried to see aspects that did not remind her of her dream. There were no bodies floating in the river today, for a start. It was also unmarred by fallen buildings. There were several half-sunken boats, and in the distance she could see a logjam of ruined craft piled against a bridge's central upright. But it was the movement of water that troubled her. Unstoppable, uncaring of what had happened in London, the water flowed towards a future she hoped she did not know.

"When do we go north?" she asked again. She'd been asking Rook the same question for the last hour, and after the first couple of times he'd stopped answering. Now he turned around and sighed, and for a moment his eyes were as black as the rooks that followed him.

"Soon," he said. "Need to see someone first."

"Who?"

"You want my help?"

Lucy-Anne nodded.

"Then let me do it my way. You don't know London, and have no idea of the dangers."

"Oh, I do have an idea, you know what happened—"

"You have no idea." He spoke softly, the words filled with such dread and certainty that Lucy-Anne could not reply. *What has he seen? What does he know?* Rook had been trapped alone in London for two years, surviving, living with the strange gift thrust upon him, and she knew so little about what his life had become, and what had come before. She silently vowed that she would find out.

"This way." Rook nodded along the embankment path, then glanced up at the summer-blue sky. Rooks floated on air currents high overhead. Others fluttered from building to building. Lucy-Anne could only see a dozen birds, but knew there must have been many more out of sight.

"Don't they give you away?" she asked.

"Most keep their distance until I need them."

"Most?"

Rook nodded up at the birds circling high overhead. "Some become so . . . obsessed that I can't shake them."

"Obsessed with you?"

Rook smiled. It was the dangerous and deadly face she had first seen, and somehow it comforted her more than the Rook mourning his lost brother. It made her feel safer.

They moved cautiously but quickly along the Thames's south bank, passing the National Theatre. Hills of litter had blown against its walls and slumped there, dampened and hardened again into a permanent addition to the building. Windows were smashed. Lucy-Anne had no wish to see what might be inside.

She wondered where her friends were now. Rook had told her they had not been caught by the Choppers, knowledge presumably imparted to him by his birds. She hoped they had escaped London. But at the same time she realised that was unlikely, because Jack would never leave without his mother and Emily. A pang of guilt hit Lucy-Anne again, the same guilt that had plagued her on and off since she'd met Rook and realised that she had abandoned her friends back in that hotel.

She'd been mad, for a time. Driven to distraction by the sudden news of her parents' demise. She should have controlled herself and borne the news better, but after two years of hope, and loneliness, and their journey into London with fresh hope drawing them all the way in, the information had been just too shattering. Somehow in her madness she had managed to sneak out of the hotel while the Choppers had been infiltrating it, and then out into the streets of London, shouting and raging at the unfairness of it all until Rook had found her. Even now she felt the dregs of that madness at the edges of her perception, and it was being nurtured by the new, terrible dreams she was experiencing. She had dreamed of Rook, and he had dreamed of her, and however much she tried to deny it she could not escape this fact.

I'm not special! she had thought, again and again. But Rook called her pure, just like his dead brother, possessing an ability

41

unconnected to what had happened to toxic London. And in truth, she'd always known there was something different about her.

When she was younger, she had experienced frequent moments of what her parents had called déjà vu. *Mummy, this has happened before . . . you picking up the phone, Daddy walking in the door, next door's dog running across the road . . .*

Déjà vu which, over time, Lucy-Anne had come to realise were dreams relived. It had troubled her little, because they had rarely concerned anything important—a phone call, a running dog. Perhaps exposed to such wonders in London, her talent was now somehow given free rein. Allowed to grow.

As for her friends . . . Her madness had given way to determination—to find Andrew—and hate it though she did, that meant that her friends were not her top priority. They would look after themselves.

"And when I've found Andrew, I'll go back to them," she said. Rook glanced back at her, but she did not elaborate. Whether he'd heard or not, he did not pass comment.

He paused by a set of stone steps, head tilted as if listening. Then he nodded and climbed, and Lucy-Anne followed. As they started crossing the long bridge spanning the Thames, Lucy-Anne could not figure out why so many people had discarded their clothes here, leaving them in rumpled piles that all seemed to trail away from a common point. Then she saw the first flash of white, and the first spread of damp dirty hair, and realised her mistake.

There must have been a hundred bodies on the bridge. They had all been running north when they fell, and some even had their arms stretched out as if to grasp the northern shore. The breeze lifted strands of hair and the flaps of rotting clothing. The corpses were mostly rotted away, leaving bones and shreds of dried skin behind.

Lucy-Anne found it sad more than shocking. So many husbands

and mothers and brothers lay here, so many children, and all of them had left someone behind.

"It's horrible," she whispered. Rook seemed surprised, but said nothing.

They crossed the bridge, and until they reached the northern shore Lucy-Anne did not look along the river at all. She glanced at the bodies she passed, and the abandoned vehicles, and imagined what those bereaved believed about the deaths of their loved ones. At the beginning they had been told the truth about the explosion at the London Eye and the release of some unknown toxic agent. But very soon after that the lies had begun. Now they were told that London was filled with the dead and would not be habitable again for a thousand years.

London Eye, Lucy-Anne thought, and then leaned against the bridge's parapet and stared along the river.

There it was. Perhaps she'd known since first stepping onto the bridge, and had been unwilling to look. But now she could see the remains of the great London Eye, the giant Ferris wheel that used to carry more than a million people annually, giving them a stunning view of London. Motionless now, the Eye was a sad echo of great, past times.

She fisted her hands, doing her best not to look away. It did not look familiar. That was a blessing, at least. In her dream, the Eye had been a mass of tumbled metal and shattered pods, but in reality it was surprisingly intact, bearing a scar towards the top where several pods had fallen away and some of the structure was bent and charred with fire.

"It's not what I saw," she whispered.

"What is it?" Rook asked.

"The Eye." She suddenly had no wish to tell him about her dream of the woman and the explosion. It felt private.

"Where it all began," he said. But he sounded uninterested, and a moment later she heard his footsteps retreating across the bridge.

Lucy-Anne looked the other way along the river, northeast towards St. Paul's. She kept her eyes wide open until they started to sting. There was no flash, no mushroom cloud consuming London. She listened to Rook retreating across the bridge behind her, knew that he would wait, and no one else appeared.

For now, Nomad remained locked away in that strange dream.

A rook landed on the parapet close to her. She took a good look at the bird, breathing softly and feeling a strong sense of purpose. She was more settled than she had been since first undertaking their journey into London, because now she knew where she was going, and why.

"Come on, then," she said to the bird. She turned to follow Rook and the bird took off, dipping low across the bridge and plucking a morsel from the gutter.

Rook was waiting at the end of the bridge, crouched low to the parapet and looking around. As she approached Lucy-Anne became more cautious, but there was no danger in his stance.

"So where are we going?" she asked.

"A museum."

"Right. Cool."

"We need to see someone." He stood from his crouch, and suddenly seemed taller than he had before, darker. *I have no idea who he is*, Lucy-Anne thought, and for the first time since fleeing her friends at the hotel she was truly afraid for herself. There was no one else around. Rook could do whatever he wanted to her, here and now, and if she fought back, he had his birds to fight for him. She had dreamed of them attacking her. *Not all dreams come true!*

"Who do we need to see?"

"Oh, her name doesn't matter. Come on."

"My brother! Andrew! You said we'd be going north to find him, and—"

"North is a big place," Rook said. "And if you think what you've seen so far is dangerous, and awful . . . well, get ready to have your eyes opened."

Unsettled by this strange boy, and with her brief madness now diluting to allow true fear to settle, Lucy-Anne followed.

Rook led them inside the London Transport Museum, looking casual but alert, and he held an entrance door open long enough for a dozen rooks to drift in past him. They moved silent as shadows, echoing his caution.

The huge building was quiet and cavernous. Rook surprised Lucy-Anne by taking her hand and guiding her across a wide walkway, glancing back and putting a finger to his lips when she tapped him on the shoulder. His grin troubled her. Not because it was frightening, but because it was . . .

It was beautiful. Her heart skipped a little. She was confused. But in truth, perhaps someone like Rook was what she had always wanted. Jack was sweet and sad and would always be one of her best friends. But he was not dangerous.

Lucy-Anne's rebellious nature had only grown deeper after Doomsday, and Rook seemed to embody everything she had wished for.

A rook landed on the boy's shoulder. He tilted his head and listened to its call.

"She's still here," he said. "Come on. Slowly. Stop when I tell you. Last time I came, she'd found a machine gun somewhere."

Lucy-Anne, still full of questions, merely listened to what Rook said and let him lead her.

In the great display hall, they moved slowly between an array of old London buses until a shadow appeared in the doorway of one.

"You come back to taunt me again, you bastard?" the woman shouted. Her voice shocked the silence, and several rooks cried out and spiralled up into the high rafters. "I'll shoot 'em! I'll blast your birds from the sky, you freak!"

"Shoot away!" Rook said, and Lucy-Anne knew that he meant it. He seemed to have no love for the birds he was so close to. She'd seen him direct hundreds of them against a helicopter's blades and engines, the resultant stew of blood, bone, and feather dropping the aircraft heavily to the ground. He'd done so without compunction, and with no sign of regret.

"Who's that with you, bird boy?"

"A friend who needs your help."

"Ha!" The woman stepped forward, and Lucy-Anne caught her first good look. She must have been fifty or sixty years old, short and thin, her hair bound with thousands of colourful beads. The gun in her hands looked ridiculously large. But she looked capable and confident, and nowhere near friendly.

"So . . . what can you do?" Lucy-Anne asked. Rook squeezed her hand hard, as if to say, *Shut up!* But the woman grimaced and raised the gun.

"Nothing for you Superior bastards," she said.

"He's not one of them," Lucy-Anne said, ignoring another squeeze from Rook. "And neither am I. I'm from outside, and I've come into London to find my brother."

"Outside," the woman said. "*Out*side?" She raised her head and took in a deep, loud breath.

Lucy-Anne felt suddenly dizzy, leaning sideways against an old vehicle and blinking at stars bursting across her vision. In the distance she heard the woman saying something, and then hands grasped her beneath the armpits and she was lowered gently to the ground.

Don't go don't go, she thought, but then her vision darkened, and all sounds receded until they were little more than echoes.

She can smell blackberries, and she looks down at her hands, expecting the familiar purple stains from when she'd used to go blackberry picking when she was a little girl. That had been when Andrew was barely a teenager and her parents had loved them both equally. But her hands show no sign of berry juice, and the sun is scorching her scalp. It is still the height of summer, the wrong time for blackberries.

She cannot not see very far because of the bushes and trees. Her surroundings are wild and overgrown, yet there is a definite sense that this was once a maintained, ordered place. A large back garden, perhaps, or a park. There is a wooden bench subsumed beneath one wall of shrubs, and a spine of coiled wire splayed across the ground, once used to mark the edge of a planting bed.

Something swings down from one of the tall trees. It is a man, naked, smeared with some sort of dye, and wearing twigs and leaves in his hair. Plant fronds seem to turn towards him as if he is a new kind of sun. He swipes at her, she ducks, and then he is away through the branches.

A woman sniffs along the ground like a clothed dog. Her nails are incredibly long, and she squats by a tree and urinates. She glances up suddenly, growls, then lopes away.

Rook appears from the shadows and rushes towards her. She knows that he is in danger, she can sense it, yet when she raises a hand to warn him back he only waves. His birds flit around him. At the last moment she finds her voice, but what emerges is a name rather than a warning.

Nomad!

The ground crumples and Rook falls into a deep pit. She hears his cry, and knows as she rushes forward that he is already dead.

What she does not expect is the sight of what is eating him.

She screams—

—and jarred awake, sitting up, panting hard, hand fisted against her chest and feeling her heart's terrified sprint.

"Calm down, calm down," a woman's voice said. It was loaded and distant.

Lucy-Anne was on the floor of an old bus, and in the seat beside her sat Rook. He only glanced at her as she caught her breath.

"What happened?" she asked.

"You fainted," the woman said. "I took you in." She was sitting on the stairs heading to the top deck, gun leaning against the wall beside her. She stared intently at Lucy-Anne.

"Took me in?" Lucy-Anne looked around, more to escape the woman's gaze than out of curiosity. It took only a moment to ascertain that the woman lived here. One double seat was piled high with a ragged assortment of clothing, another with blankets and pillows. There were plastic bottles filled with water, tins of food, and farther along the bus she thought she saw a pile of stuffed toys peering over the metal railing of a seat's back.

"Yeah," the woman said. "Hey."

Lucy-Anne looked back at her.

"You're seventeen," the woman said. "Looked after yourself since Doomsday. No virgin, but you haven't loved for a while. Time of the month in . . ." she shrugged. "Six days." Her eyes narrowed and she glanced aside, displaying the first sign of emotion. "You just found out your parents are dead."

"And my brother's alive!" Lucy-Anne said. "That's why Rook brought me here, because you can help."

"Somewhere to the north," Rook said.

"Yes. The north. And you'll not want to find him," the woman said. "Better off dead. Ever heard that saying, girl? I think it all the time, but don't have the fucking guts. Huh."

"Lucy-Anne, meet the charming Sara."

"I *do* want to find him!" Lucy-Anne said. "And if you know where he is you have to—"

"Have to nothing," Sara said. She stood and climbed the stairs, disappearing quickly from sight.

"What is this?" Lucy-Anne asked.

"She can scent information," Rook said.

"So she can sniff out Andrew?"

"I think she already did."

Lucy-Anne stood and started up the stairs, ignoring Rook's half-hearted attempt to call her back. *He fell he was down the hole he wouldn't listen when I called.* On the top deck she paused and looked around in surprise.

Every seat was taken by a shop mannequin. They were all dressed, some extravagantly, others in jeans and tee shirts. She couldn't help feeling every eye upon her.

"You met Nomad," Sara said. She was sitting three seats along the bus, a plastic man beside her sporting a running top and waterproof coat.

"No," Lucy-Anne said.

"Sounds like you did. *Smells* like you did."

"Only in my dreams."

"Hmph." Sara looked her up and down. "You're an odd one. That hair, those clothes. And from outside. I didn't think . . . didn't let myself believe that outside existed anymore. There's just London, and death, and sometimes one becomes the other. Interchangeable. It's not a nice place."

"Tell me about it," Lucy-Anne said. And when Sara seemed to take that as a cue to talk, she did not interrupt.

"He *is* to the north. Hampstead Heath, or whatever it's called now. But, girl . . . that's a dead place. You think London's bad, that's somewhere else. Removed by what it's become." She nodded at the stairs. "Even those so-called Superiors don't venture there. It's a no-go place, and if *you* go there, you'll die."

"What's there?"

"Bad people, hungry and cruel."

"I'm going anyway."

Sara watched her, suddenly growing immensely sad. "I had a daughter, few years older than you. She'd moved away a couple of years before Doomsday, we'd had a row, hadn't talked in over a year. I wonder . . ." She stared into space, then turned to look at the mannequin beside her. Perhaps she talked to them. Maybe they were her family now.

Unable to think of anything comforting to say, Lucy-Anne descended the stairs to find Rook still sitting where she'd left him.

"Hampstead Heath," she said, and his dark expression only echoed what Sara had said. Lucy-Anne didn't care. She was going, and she knew that Rook was intrigued enough to accompany her.

She tried to forget seeing him fall. *Not all dreams come true.*

CHAPTER FOUR
PRISONERS

As soon as Jenna could not open the door, Jack knew that they were in trouble.

"Now what?" Sparky said. He stood and rattled at the handle, as if his own strength could undo it when Jenna's could not.

"It's locked, Dumbo," Jenna said.

"Yeah? Watch this." Sparky took two steps back and braced himself, ready to shoulder-bash the door and probably break a bone in the process.

"Sparky!" Jack said. His friend paused, then relaxed.

"They've probably got a guard out there," Jenna said.

"So what the hell's going on?" Sparky asked.

"Me," Jack said. "Breezer wants to see what's happening to me."

"And what is?" Jenna asked softly.

"A change," Jack said. He searched for something else to say, to explain, but he could not. Tears threatened. "I'm really scared, guys."

"Still a pussy," Sparky said. But he clapped Jack on the shoulder, then ruffled his hair like a parent comforting a kid.

"So how do we get out of this one?" Jenna asked.

"Yeah," Sparky said. "Can't you, like, magic the door open, or something?" Jenna nudged him in the ribs, and he feigned hurt. He pinched her rump, she slapped his face.

Jack turned away, pursed his lips, thinking. He felt a flush of anger at Breezer—he'd taken them in to protect them, now he held them prisoner—but the man was only doing what he thought was best. That didn't mean he could be reasoned with.

And there was no guarantee he would not use physical force to keep them there.

"This is an office block, not a prison," Jack said. "Thin walls. Plasterboard. We know there's probably someone watching the door out there." He turned around and pointed at the wall behind him. "So we go that way."

"Huh?" Sparky asked.

Jack pulled the folding knife from his pocket and flipped open the blade. He scored a long, deep line down the wall from face to waist height, and a drift of fine plaster fell out onto the bare concrete floor. He glanced back at Sparky and Jenna, grinning.

"Won't take long."

Jenna pulled her own knife and started two feet along the wall from Jack. They worked gently and deliberately, until Jack held up a hand and bent to look through the cut he'd formed. It was pitch back, but he realised it was a double-sided partition.

With a soft shove, Sparky pushed out and pulled away the section they'd outlined and set it aside, exposing metal studding and the back side of the opposite wall surface.

Twenty minutes later he pulled out a second square of plasterboard. *Let this be easy*, Jack thought, and they all held their breath.

The room beyond was much like the sparse office they had been locked into, except that the door stood ajar. Beyond, the sunlit corridor.

"Quietly," Jack said.

"Slowly, slowly, catchee monkey," Sparky whispered, lifting himself up through the hole.

Moments later they were in the second office. Jack felt time ticking by. *Breezer will be waiting to talk to us, persuade us to his way of thinking. He'll be keen to see me again, because it's me he's interested in.* He felt a flush of pity for Breezer, but he was more and more determined—his mother and Emily came first, and Reaper was the only sure way to rescue them alive.

London, the survivors, the Choppers, the lies being fed to the public, even his own strange, growing powers . . . they all came second.

Jack peeked into the corridor. A man sat on the floor outside the door to the room they had just left. He had no weapon, and looked harmless. But the longer they avoided detection, the better their chances at escape. So far Breezer had only locked a door; there was no saying how much farther he would go to keep Jack from fleeing.

Jack moved back from the door and pressed his fingers to his lips. Jenna and Sparky nodded, eyes wide as they watched their friend. Jack knew they would always be a little afraid of him now, and he could hardly blame them. He was a little afraid of himself.

He delved inside, sensing for the star-scape of his burgeoning powers. They were chaotic and uneven, a miasma of possibilities, and suddenly he was confused. If he touched this star, what would happen? Who would he hurt, who would he kill? *If I make the wrong choice, might I become like my father?* He reached out but withdrew again, trying to sense his way through this troubling constellation.

This one. He grasped a spark and pulled back, and as Jenna took his arm and he slumped, he could sense the strong pulsing of her heart and the flow and ebb of her life force.

"Wrong one," Jack said. "It's . . . no . . . wrong one. Hang on, I . . ."

"We've all got special powers," Sparky said. He pulled something from his pocket, glanced outside, then flicked it along the corridor.

Jack heard a small metal *clang*, then Sparky turned to the two of them. "Got maybe ten seconds," he whispered, and he pulled the door open.

Jenna hauled Jack upright as Sparky slipped through the door and across the corridor. By the time Jack and Jenna stood by the open doorway, Sparky was holding open the door to the staircase, beckoning them over.

Jenna pulled Jack out and he had to follow, treading lightly, clasping her hand, only glancing to his right as he felt the coolness of the stairwell embracing him.

The man was fifteen feet along the corridor, his back to them and head tilted. He had yet to find the coin, take a while to think about that, unlock the door, check inside the office, find them gone—

"Now maybe we've got half a minute," Sparky whispered as he eased the door closed. "Come on!"

They started down the staircase, and it reminded Jack of fleeing that terrible hotel only days before. Then he had seen a man have his head blown off, grenades had exploded, and Jenna had been shot in the stomach. It was only Rosemary and her healer friend who had saved Jenna, delving inside her for the bullet and then knitting her wounds from the inside out.

If one of them was injured now, there was no one to help.

No one but me, Jack thought. But his fledgling powers still confused and scared him. He felt like a Neanderthal man given access to Apple's research and development department. He had toyed with some powers, but maybe that had been a fluke.

Maybe the powers were toying with him.

Jack reckoned they had about fifteen floors to descend. That was thirty flights of stairs. On the ground floor there would doubtless be someone keeping watch, but they would tackle that problem when they got there.

Sparky led the way, taking each flight in four long strides, then crouching on the landings and half landings, listening, before heading off again. Jenna seemed to flow rather than walk, her natural grace giving her stealth and fitness. Jack panted from exertion and fear. He was worried for himself, but more worried for Sparky and Jenna. Breezer claimed not to be a Superior, but there was no saying how he'd treat Jack's friends if they were recaptured. It was Jack he was interested in.

And Superior, Irregular . . . they were only names. Actions made a person, not what they chose to call themselves.

As Sparky jumped three steps onto a landing a door opened, and a man with bright ginger hair stepped through. He was carrying a tray of cups and bottled water, balanced on one hand while the other held the door open.

He looked at Sparky, his expression one of complete shock.

"Ha!" Sparky said.

The man drew in a breath to shout and Sparky punched him in the mouth. He dropped the tray and staggered back against the door jamb, banging his head and crying out.

"Sparky!" Jenna said, but Sparky ignored her and punched the man again. He went down in a heap. His splayed legs kicked cups across the landing, and they passed beneath the railings and clattered down the stairwell, shattering, skittering across concrete. There could not have been a more effective alarm.

"Karl?" a voice called.

Sparky looked back and forth between Jack and the fallen man.

"Came from down there," Jenna said, stepping back from the railing.

Sparky pointed through the door. The fallen man was moaning, holding his mouth, shaking his dazed head slowly, and his crumpled body held the door open.

"We go through there and we'll be trapped on this floor," Jack whispered.

"Karl? What's happening. You all right?" Footsteps from below, at least three sets, rapidly climbing. Shattered crockery was kicked aside.

Breezer had said they had escape routes from above as well. Zip wire? Window cleaners' cradle? Jack didn't know. But right then it seemed the best idea. It was away from pursuit, it kept them in the stairwell . . . and no one would expect them to do something so foolish.

"Up," Jack whispered, gesturing with his thumb. He turned and started climbing, not waiting for his friends' objections. Eight steps up he paused and glanced back. Sparky and Jenna were frozen there, and the fallen man was swaying on hands and knees, spitting blood.

"Trust me," Jack said.

It took a minute to draw level with the door to the floor they'd escaped, and Jack sprinted past it, expecting it to burst open at any second. He heard shouting from below—more than one voice now—and he feared what they might use against them. Would they freeze their muscles, steal their air, make their blood boil? He sought the memory of Nomad so that he could access his own sparks of power, but the running and fear conspired to confuse him. All he had was what he'd always had—himself. That would have to be good enough.

They ran, and doors burst open below them.

"Jack, you'll doom us all!" Breezer shouted. Jack slowed on a landing and glanced back, but Sparky and Jenna were right behind him, faces stern as they shook their heads.

"We're away now, mate," Sparky said.

"Door." Jenna nodded past Jack, and they found themselves on the final landing facing a bolted steel door. The padlock was heavy, but hung open.

"Escape route," Jack said.

"But to where?" Sparky asked.

Jack knocked the padlock aside and pushed the door open. There was a dark boiler room beyond, and a small hooped ladder leading up to a ceiling hatch.

"What, do heights scare you as much as chickens?" Jack asked.

"Squaw! Squaw!" Jenna said, flapping her arms as she pushed past Jack and setting the three of them laughing. Nervous, panicked laughter, but it felt good nonetheless. Jack felt a rush of intense love for his friends.

"Sparky, padlock," he said as he slipped through the door. Sparky picked up the padlock and followed, and then they slammed the door closed.

Even through the metal they could hear footsteps pounding up the staircase beyond.

"Couple of floors down, do you reckon?" Sparky asked.

"Yeah. Jenna, get the trap opened." Jack glanced back and saw that she was already there, forcing back bolts and opening the trap, sunlight flooding the room like a burst of hope. Jenna stuck her head up through the trap.

"Oh, shit," she said.

"What?" Jack called. He was frantically scanning the door, searching for a hasp and staple through which to lock the padlock.

"You guys are gonna love this."

"Go!" Jack said, shoving Sparky towards the ladder.

"Don't be stupid," Sparky said, and in those words was complete understanding. It was Jack they wanted, and Jack who was important here. "Jack, what you did to me."

"Huh?"

"The heat. Made me sweat." Sparky tapped the door's handle. "Never know."

Jack frowned, sensed inside for the power he had used on Sparky . . . and found it, as available to him as speech or thought. He pointed at the door's lock and concentrated, thinking the metal hot, thinking the catch orange and molten.

"Shit!" Sparky said, backing up to the ladder. "Mate, I can feel that heat. You could have melted the bollocks off me!"

"Could have," Jack said, smiling.

Footsteps thundered up the stairs beyond the door, and Jack was about to shout a warning when he heard a scream. Someone had grasped the handle. They wouldn't do so again anytime soon. Jack felt a twinge of guilt, but then he pointed again and concentrated some more. It was a strange feeling, as if heat formed in his mind and left him untouched, flowing across the space between his hand and the door and super-heating the metal. He had the idea that he could melt the door if he really wanted. He could turn it to gas. The power was startling and frightening, but he felt fully in control of it. He *could* have melted the bollocks off Sparky . . . but he'd chosen not to.

"Yeah," Jack breathed, flushed with the power.

"Come on!" Sparky whispered. "Jenna was right. You're gonna love this."

"Sorry!" Jack shouted through the door, and then the banging began.

Up the ladder and out onto the rooftop, Jack slammed the hatch shut again before standing and joining his friends.

"You've gotta be kidding," he said.

"Nope," Jenna said.

Sparky seemed delighted. "Cool. Cool!"

There were three hang gliders on the roof. Two were folded and dismantled, but one appeared to be fully assembled, its wheels and wings tied down to prevent any errant breezes from stealing it away. A single seat was suspended beneath it. Twenty feet from its front wheel, a section of railing had been cut away to allow launch.

"Have you ever . . . ?" Jack asked, but he didn't need to finish.

He knew that neither of his friends had ever done anything like this. That didn't stop Sparky. He delved into Jenna's jeans pocket, blowing her a kiss as he probed for her penknife.

"Come on!" he said. "Got seconds. Come on!"

"Maybe we should . . ." Jenna said.

"Wait?" Jack asked. He could still hear banging from the plant room beneath them as they tried to break through the door and its super-heated catch. "There won't be another chance. They catch us, and Breezer will make sure we won't get away again."

"Yeah, but this?" Jenna pointed at the aircraft Sparky was freeing. Four cuts from the sharp knife and he was wheeling it towards the roof's edge, looking back at them expectantly.

"Breezer wants me," Jack said. "Jenna, I'm afraid what he might do to you two."

"He's no monster. Not like . . ."

"Reaper? Dunno. We just don't know."

Something changed below them. The banging ceased, and then a different sound came—the metal door swinging open and impacting the wall.

"Come on!" Sparky shouted. He was already jumping into the seat.

"For Mum," Jack said. "For Emily." He grabbed Jenna's arm and ran across the rooftop to the hang glider.

He'd once taken a trip to South Wales to visit relatives with his parents. It was soon after Emily was born, and he remembered eating an ice cream in a car park in Abergavenny and watching dark specks drifting down from a hilltop in the distance. They'd waited in that car park long enough to see the first giant winged shape grow larger and pass almost overhead, heading for a field by the river which was their favoured landing point. There had been one person strapped into the seat. Only one.

"This isn't a bloody passenger aircraft," Jack said, but Jenna was already pushing. Sparky was braced in the seat, lifting himself up so that the straps that should have held him in splayed to either side.

"Close enough," he said. He was breathing fast, excitement and fear, and Jack closed his eyes for a moment. Just a second, to gather himself.

He was terrified.

They were twenty floors above the ground. If he'd taken time to look he could have identified a handful of buildings and landmarks, but he felt sick to the pit of his stomach. They didn't have a clue what they were doing, whether this thing was air-worthy, whether three of them would be too heavy and it would plunge to the ground. Maybe Breezer was waiting at a window a few floors below even now, someone else with him ready to fold wings or snap struts with their mind.

If he can't have me, maybe he'd rather see me dead, Jack thought.

But then Sparky was dragging them the last few feet to the edge of the roof with his feet, and Jack and Jenna jumped onto fibreglass struts on either side of the bucket seat, wrapped their arms around framing, and grasped the loose straps.

"Bloody hell," Sparky muttered as the front wheel dropped over the edge of the building.

"Yeah," Jack said.

They fell.

Jack had never been so scared. The aircraft's frame shook and rattled, the canvas wing snapped and slapped, the wind blasted against his face and took his breath away and blurred his vision, and they were plummeting towards the ground, nose dipped down and the vehicle-strewn street rapidly approaching.

"Pull it up!" Jack shouted, but his words were stolen away.

Jenna was hugging the strut, eyes squeezed shut, strap twisted around her arm and biting into her skin so hard that blood dribbled, whipped away by the wind.

Jack leaned in towards Sparky, not daring to let go, and shouted again. "Sparky!"

Sparky turned to look at Jack, eyes wide and his spiked blond hair pressed flat across his head.

"Pull . . . up!"

Sparky nodded and grabbed the control handles. They were linked via wires and metal connectors to the wing above them, and though Jack had no idea how it worked, there must have been some element of control. Sparky pulled the handles, and immediately their nose rose, almost flipping them up onto their back.

If that happens we'll stall and then just fall, Jack thought, and he risked letting go of the strut. He fell forward across Sparky's arm and grabbed one controller, easing back and feeling Sparky's immediate understanding. The hang glider levelled . . . and then they were drifting, and flying.

"Yeaaaahhhh!" Sparky screamed.

Jenna's eyes opened a crack, then squeezed shut again.

As if finding its own level, the aircraft suddenly stopped shaking, and the breeze pressing against Jack's face lessened. He still gripped tight, but for a moment he felt safer. Safe enough at least to glance around, see where they were heading, and spot a hundred dangers in their path.

They'd dropped at least half the building's height before levelling out, and now other buildings loomed, and aerials on lower structures reached for them.

Jack looked back, but they were already too far away from Breezer's skyscraper to make out any details.

"Got to make some distance!" Jack shouted. Sparky nodded

once, all his concentration on the control handles. Jack could see his friend tweaking the handles here and there, muscles in his arms flexing and his brow furrowed as he slowly got the feel of the aircraft. The glider dipped and rose, and then as they drifted to the left and approached a bland grey concrete and glass monolith, they rose and barely passed above it.

Sparky beamed in delight. Jenna opened her eyes once more, then closed them again.

"We're okay!" Jack shouted to her, but she merely pressed her lips tighter together.

They passed over a green square with several bombed-out buildings marring its northern side. Jack wondered at their story. Shapes moved across the square's overgrown lawns, pale faces looking up, and he tried to make out what they were wearing—royal blue Choppers, or the more rag-tag clothing of London's survivors—but they passed overhead too quickly. If there were voices or gunshots, the wind swallowed them.

Jack closed his eyes and tried to sense back the way they had come, but he could not grasp any power that enabled him to do so. The potential within him was staggering, but much of his fear came from his erratic ability to source it at will.

"We're flying!" Sparky shouted. He let his natural exuberance loose, whooping and shouting, but always maintaining gentle control.

Jack could not help grinning. Ask nine out of ten people what their secret power would be, and they'd say flying. He'd not yet seen or heard of anyone in London who could do this unaided—and he doubted he ever would, because Evolve seemed to have worked more on minds than on bodies—but this was as near as it could be. They *were* flying, and for the first time since entering London through tunnels and sewers, Jack felt completely free.

And yet . . .

He looked down at the roofs and streets passing below, and the parks and squares, abandoned vehicles, gardens, storage units, and factories, and then the River Thames . . . and all the while he felt watched.

But these were not Nomad's eyes.

"Let's put it down!" Jack shouted.

"Er . . ." Sparky said. "Right. Yeah. Down."

Jenna kept her eyes squeezed shut and maintained the same position, and Jack thought it best to leave her until they had landed.

He scanned ahead and below them, trying to spot a safe landing site, trying also not to think about their combined weight this thing was not meant to carry and the impact they might suffer on striking the ground.

As if responding to his doubts the hang glider dropped suddenly, Jack's stomach turning, Sparky shouting, and from his right Jack heard Jenna's low, pained groan.

Sparky fought with the controls, tongue sticking from the corner of his mouth as he concentrated on steering them away from the face of a department store, then edging them to the left again as a tall aerial loomed atop an office building. The aerial slapped the aircraft a foot from Jack's leg, smashing a strut into fibreglass shards. They lurched, then started banking to the left.

"Going down on the road," Sparky shouted.

"Watch out for the bus!"

Sparky did not reply, too busy concentrating. Jack held on tight. He had brief visions of the wheels disintegrating, the aircraft coming apart, and the three of them rolling and scraping across the tarmac, slamming against vehicles or buildings, their broken, dead bodies eventually rotting where they came to rest. He did not believe they were destined for such a pointless ending, and yet he was only too aware of the vagaries of fate.

The wheels struck the ground and they bounced, twisting to the left, striking again, and during the second bounce Sparky twisted them to the right, ensuring that the next impact took them past a bus slewed across the road. The front wheel struck the kerb, but by then their speed had drastically lessened.

Jack let himself roll ahead of the hang glider. As he came to rest on the pavement he took a moment's pause, looking up at the clear blue sky and enjoying the brief silence.

"Thank you for flying Sparky Airways," Sparky said. "Please ensure you have all your belongings. Apologies for the bumpy landing. I can confirm that the pilot shit himself."

Jack sat up and grinned at his friend. Sparky smiled back, then shrugged as if it was nothing.

"All in a day's work, eh?" Jack asked.

Jenna was slowly releasing the strut and unwinding the strap from around her arm. She wiped absently at where it had chaffed her skin raw, smearing blood, then stood on the solid ground. Her knees bent a little, and when she reached out for balance Sparky grabbed her hand. She nodded, stood upright, and looked around, as if only just waking from a deep sleep.

"Jenna?" Sparky asked.

"Sparky," she said, her voice a croak. "If you ever do that again, I'll slit your throat in your sleep." Then she let go of his hand, turned around, and vomited on the pavement.

Jack frowned and stood. And even though his girlfriend was puking, Sparky saw Jack's expression, and recognised that something was wrong.

"What?" Sparky asked.

"Ever feel like you're being watched?" Jack asked. He scanned their surroundings—the bus slewed across the street, other cars parked along the road on flat tyres, the silent façades of buildings on both sides. Shopfronts were smashed, burnt out, or the windows were dusty and dirty, hiding anyone or anything that might be watching from inside. A pavement café was a mass of overturned timber tables and rusted chairs. Along the street, an Underground entrance was a burnt-out mess, as if a great fire had belched from beneath London. The taint of fire was still on the air. A breeze rustled litter along the street. Dark circles of chewing gum speckled the pavement around him. He saw and sensed all these things, yet the overriding sensation was of being observed.

And it was *not* Nomad. Her memory in his mind was already a familiar feeling. This was something else. Something *other*.

"All the time," Jenna said. She seemed a little better, and was allowing Sparky to hold her upright, one arm around her waist.

"No," Jack said. "By someone particular."

"This one of your powers?" Sparky asked.

Jack shook his head, though he was unsure. "Sixth sense."

"Prickly-neck feeling," Jenna said.

"Yeah," Sparky said. "Tingly balls."

"We should be moving," Jack said. "We covered, what, a mile?"

"I reckon two," Sparky said.

"So we put more distance between us before we take a rest," Jack said.

"And you know how to find your father?" Jenna asked.

"I'll figure it out," Jack said.

He saw the look passing between Sparky and Jenna, and turned away. He was already feeling more distant from his friends, and not because of their growing closeness. He was becoming more and more different.

"Come on," he said. "Let's run." Jack led the way. They passed the bus and a wrecked van hidden behind it, and Jack caught a glimpse of a dead face following him from the driver's window. He gasped with shock, then saw the hollow gaze of a skull. It had been picked clean by carrion creatures and it leaned against the window frame, grinning as they ran by.

Perhaps the bus was full with passengers who would never arrive at their destination. He had no wish to see.

He heard his friends' footsteps behind him. As he ran he tried to analyse the sense he had of being watched, and why it felt so strong. This was not a new power, he was certain. Perhaps it was merely a self-perpetuating idea that became more definite the more he thought of it.

As they approached a confluence of three roads he was looking up at the buildings, some windows smashed and some dusty and closed, searching for the face of their watcher. Doing so meant that he didn't see the Choppers.

"Jack!" Sparky shouted.

There were three blue-painted vehicles powering along a road towards them, each of them large enough to hold six Choppers. The front vehicle, a Jeep, bore a heavy angled plough, and it shoved an abandoned BMW convertible aside with barely a pause.

They were a hundred yards away when brakes screamed, and the windscreen of the Jeep shattered into a glittering, blood-red haze.

CHAPTER FIVE
THE NORTH

Lucy-Anne's fascination with Rook was growing by the minute. And though she was seeing some terrible things, she could not deny that she was also enjoying her adventure. *That's mad*, she thought. *This isn't an adventure, it's a disaster.* But she was happy to deny her inner voice.

"What's your story?" she asked him as they left the Transport Museum.

"Mine?" Rook looked at her in surprise.

"I'm putting my trust in you," Lucy-Anne said. "You're taking me into the north of London."

"I haven't said I would yet," he said, but the ensuing silence between them spoke volumes. She already knew that he was interested in her. Now she wanted to know why.

"This way," he said, nodding along the street. "Let's keep moving and I'll tell you as much as I . . ." He started walking, and Lucy-Anne followed. Rooks drifted above them, like shadows of a shattered night. *Much as I want to?* she thought. *Or as much as I remember?*

"I was living in Collier's Wood with my mother. Dad left a few years ago. Met a stripper in Soho, fell in love, took her to live in Cornwall." He grinned without humour. "Sordid, eh?"

Lucy-Anne did not reply. She was finding it strange enough imagining Rook with a mother, living in a house. Something normal for this extraordinary boy.

"When Doomsday hit, me and David were on the way home

from school. We'd stopped at a pizza place and were eating with some friends. Heard about an explosion at the Eye, didn't think much of it. Bit of a shock, but we were just kids, you know? There've been bombs before. So we were just eating and messing around, and then we left and started for home. There was me and David, and . . ." He frowned, shrugged. "A few friends. Can't remember their names anymore.

"It wasn't 'til we passed Collier's Wood tube station that we saw something weird. Loads of people rushing from the tube. They all looked scared, panicked. Most of them were on their phones, not looking where they were going or communicating with anyone around them. A fat guy was hit by a car. No one stopped, no one seemed to care. So we took off towards our street, our friends tagged along—they lived past the end of our street, usually came into our place for a play on the Wii or something after school. At the end of the street, they just . . . dropped. Hit the pavement. One second they were walking with us, the next they fell."

He was silent for a while, and Lucy-Anne tried to imagine this strange, deadly boy playing computer games and walking home from school with friends. They were such mundane activities that she could not make the connection. But Rook's expression made it for her; she had never seen him looking so human.

"A load of pigeons gathered on the rooftops took flight and flew in tight circles above us, like living tornadoes. David looked terrified. I knew it was him—I'd known for a while about what he could do, or some of it—but he'd always been afraid. I reached for him to . . . hold his hand, or something. But they were falling everywhere. Along the street from us two cars crashed head-on, and another flipped over onto its back and smashed down the front wall of a house. There was a really big explosion, and screaming, and then my vision started blurring. David grabbed my hand. I passed out." Rook held up one hand as if to illustrate his brother's touch, but then Lucy-Anne realised that he had called a halt. A rook drifted down to land on his shoulder, he tilted his head, and the bird took off again.

"It's okay," he said. "Irregulars. Come on." They walked on, past the entrance to an indoor market and a jeweller's with rings and necklaces still scattered on the pavement amongst broken glass. Lucy-Anne looked around but saw no one watching them. Whoever it was the birds had seen must have been hiding.

"What happened when you woke up?"

"Everyone was dead," Rook said. "It was like . . . waking in another world. London was mostly quiet. Some shouts, screams, from a couple of people stumbling about. We never saw any, though. I suppose we were lucky. We had each other. So we went home. And our mother was dead. Sitting in her armchair, and the TV was still on, then. An advert for washing powder. Her cup of tea was still warm.

"After that things are hazy. Time seems weird. We stayed together, I know that. Outside was terrifying and horrible. So *silent*, and when there were voices, they were screaming or mad. It might have been a couple of days or three weeks, living in our house almost as normal. David made food, washed up, and we dressed in clean clothes every day. And when the TV and radio were off, and the Internet couldn't connect anymore, and David's mobile had no signal and after we'd buried Mum in the back garden, under the thornless rose bush she'd planted by the back gate so that we didn't prick ourselves on it when we were little . . . after that, when we *did* start thinking about leaving, a man told us not to."

"A man?" Lucy-Anne prompted when he seemed to drift off.

"A black man. He looked like he was a hundred years old. I think I'd seen him before, selling flowers at the local market on Saturday mornings. He came down our street at nine forty-three every morning. Same time, exactly. He called himself a crier, like an old town crier, you know? And he told us to stay where we were, because everything was terrible. Told us stories. We didn't believe them, of course."

"What sort of stories?"

"I'm sure you can guess." He stopped walking and looked at a swathe of graffiti across a shop's side wall. It was a strange mixture of symbols and images, as if written in an alien language.

"So we stayed at home, and then I discovered that I could . . ." Rook waved one hand around his head, and seven rooks circled above them for a few moments before drifting apart once more. "It was amazing to me, and strange to David. His own powers were so much greater than they'd been before, and he couldn't handle it. The day the black man didn't come, David went out. He was picked up by the Choppers."

"Do you know what happened to him?" she asked. Rook glanced back at her, his eyes hard, and Lucy-Anne realised that she'd asked an intensely personal question. If he did know, and it was as awful as she feared, then she had no right asking him to relive it.

"They killed him," Rook said.

"You . . ." She trailed off, unsure.

"What?"

"You're sure?" she asked quietly. "Only . . . maybe the Choppers were trying to help. In the beginning, at least."

Rook walked to the kerb and stopped, as if waiting for the motionless traffic to start moving again. "You think?"

"Well, maybe. At first. I mean, I know what they do now. We've heard the stories, and everything. But I just don't want to believe they were doing that right at the start."

"Really?" He stared at her, then his expression softened a little. "I only wish you could see."

"See what?"

"What my rooks show me. They saw. They followed him, because my powers were young, unformed, chaotic. It was David they were for back then, as well as all the other birds. But it was only the rooks that came back to me and shared what they saw. The Choppers grabbed him from a supermarket where he was trying to break in to get food. They bundled him into the back of a van, slit his throat, collected as much of his blood as they could. Then they cut off the top of his head and took out his brain."

Lucy-Anne blinked at Rook, unable to break his gaze.

"The birds left him, then. Dead, by the Choppers' hands."

"And you've been avenging him ever since," she whispered. It was dreadful—this poor kid, barely older than her, made into a vessel of vengeance. A killer.

"In a way," he said. "I accepted right away that he was gone, because I already knew that I was changing, and the rooks were no mystery to me. I was becoming more like he'd been, for whatever reason. But it's more as if I was trying to bring him back. And now, with you . . ."

"With me?"

"Someone else special," Rook said, stepping forward and touching her face. "Touched before Doomsday. Pure."

"Oh, I'm not pure," Lucy-Anne said, shivering at his touch.

"I've been waiting for you ever since David died."

"And Reaper? The Superiors?"

Rook smiled, a terrible expression. "What I do serves them, and they can sometimes help me."

"You feel nothing for those Choppers you killed?"

"They're not people anymore," he said. "They're from outside. Another world."

"So am I."

"Yes. But you belong *here*." He turned away from her and started

71

walking again, and just for a moment Lucy-Anne felt under intense scrutiny. She looked up and saw several rooks sitting on window sills, a few more circling gently above, and every single one of them was gazing down at her. Their eyes, black and lifeless. Then they took flight to follow Rook, like dregs of his own psyche blown apart by Doomsday. Perhaps everything he did was an attempt to hold himself together.

Later that afternoon Rook suggested that they rest in a house for a while. He said that moving farther north during the day was dangerous, and that entering the wilder parts of London would be better achieved under cover of darkness.

"Isn't that when whatever's there comes out?" Lucy-Anne asked.

"What, like vampires?" Rook was mocking her, but she would not rise to his bait.

"It's just that night always feels more dangerous. And don't birds sleep at night?"

"Not mine," he said. "They do what I ask of them, whenever I ask. They'll guide us in, and we'll be shadows. Darkness will hide us."

The house Rook broke into had probably once been worth a million pounds, but now its fine furnishings and tasteful decor held no value when it came to survival. They tramped dirty shoes across cream carpet, and he told her to wait in the living room while he checked the rest of the house.

Several rooks had entered the house with them, and one perched on the back of an easy chair, watching Lucy-Anne. She hoped she was being protected, but suspected it was more likely that she was being guarded.

Trying not to look at the bird—it was unnaturally motionless, eyes reflecting nothing—she glanced around at the room, attempting to connect with the family that had once owned this place. She skimmed over the furniture, the paintings, the ornaments and photographs, because they were more a part of the house than whoever had used to live here. The objects that did affect her were those that spoke of a human touch. On the bookshelf, an open book lay face-down, never to be finished. On the floor beneath a small table, a children's toy car gathered dust, its brash redness subdued by time. A sheaf of papers sat on the table. A coat was draped across the back of the sofa, and a wallet hung half-out of the inner pocket. Half-finished things that would never be taken up by their owners again. They made her sad.

Rook reappeared in the doorway, and the watching bird fluttered past him and from the room with hardly a sound.

"Family's upstairs," he said, glancing around the room. "We'll stay down here. Two sofas. I'll check the kitchen, see if any canned food's still edible."

Lucy-Anne only nodded, and as he left again she leaned across so that she could see the staircase outside. She felt no temptation to go up.

As she heard Rook rooting through the kitchen cupboards she sat back in the sofa and breathed in deeply. She'd had one night's disturbed sleep since leaving her friends, and exhaustion was creeping in. Sleep lured her down, yet Andrew urged her on.

"I will find you," she whispered, and the room seemed to be listening. But what *would* she find? In the north of London, where even people like Rook chose not to tread and there were bad people, hungry and cruel, would the Andrew she might find be one that she wanted?

A flutter, and three rooks entered the room. They perched in high corners and became as motionless as shadows.

She remembered him from when they were younger and tried to imagine what he might be capable of now.

Her eyes drooped. When she jerked in her sleep and looked

again, one of the rooks had come closer, standing motionless on a low coffee table not six feet from her. She stared, it stared back. She lifted one foot quickly, as if to kick out, but the bird did not move. *He's watching me*, she thought.

The sofa was deep and soft. From the kitchen, she heard the dull rasp of a tin being opened, and then something wet being spooned into a bowl.

Between blinks the bird vanished from sight and the room lit up, suddenly bright and airy and filled with life once more.

Rook is there before her, sitting in a chair and drinking from a steaming mug. He's smiling, and there is no mockery in that expression now, no superiority. He starts to stand and—

Music is playing through the room's stereo system. It's something soft and gentle, lulling. Rook sits on the sofa beside her, and though they do not live here, she feels very much at home. She glances at the window, where net curtains are hung to conceal the view outside. She leans sideways, because between curtains and window there is a chink of bare glass, and she thinks perhaps she has seen an eye—

She is lying on the sofa and Rook is sitting by her side. She's all but naked. Rook's smile is both alluring and comforting, as if this has all happened before. She glances at the window, but the curtains have been drawn tightly closed.

The toy car is no longer beneath the table. The book has been closed and re-shelved. The coat over the back of the sofa is now Rook's, and the wallet hanging from the inside pocket is spilling ink-black feathers.

She opens her mouth, but Rook kisses her—

Rook is lying on her, and when she looks past him the room is filled with rooks, perching on the picture rail, the bookshelves, the table and the backs of chairs. As she opens her mouth to cry out they beat her to it, *caw-caw*ing as one, flapping their wings and suddenly filling the space with frantic movement.

Lucy-Anne shouted herself awake, sitting up on the sofa, waving her hands around her head to ward off the birds and push Rook away. But she was alone in the room once more, and any watching birds had gone.

Rook rushed into the room, looking around for any threat. "What?" he asked.

Lucy-Anne pressed one had to her chest. Her heart was beating hard. She shook her head.

"Dream?" he asked.

"Yeah." She did not elaborate. How could she?

"Was this one about me, too?" he asked, smiling. Then he held up one finger and turned, leaving the room and calling back, "Food in one minute!"

Lucy-Anne stood and paced the room. She stood by the window and moved the closed curtains aside, revealing bare glass and no net curtains. Outside, the street was silent and motionless. There was no sense of being watched.

"What the bloody hell?" she muttered. Whether the dream was prophecy or desire, there was no way to know. But for a moment it had all felt so real.

Drawn like a searcher to a beacon in the dark, Nomad drifted through the streets of London.

I have felt this before, and touched him, and now Jack is just beginning to understand his potential. But this . . .

Nomad usually wandered, yet now she moved with unaccustomed purpose. She sensed other people seeing her and moving out of the way. Eyes followed her progress, and whispers sounded behind her, wrapping her in myth and legend.

As she approached her target, she probed with inhuman senses, constructing a picture of what she would see and why she was being impelled this way. She paused by a knot of crashed and burned vehicles.

I have felt this before, but this time is different.

Soon, she saw the girl. Purple-haired, strong, angry, confused, she was accompanied by a boy and his birds. They were heading north, searching for her brother, whom Nomad could have found if she so desired. But she did not yet wish that. She had come to learn that leaving matters to fate might sometimes steer the world.

She watched them from the shadow of a doorway, and when the girl saw her watching she froze, scared and confused.

And Nomad gasped.

She had seen this girl in dreadful dreams she did her best to forget.

The girl ran at her and Nomad quickly melted away, fleeing through buildings and across roads, down alleys and up staircases. Behind her, she sensed the girl's confusion.

Nomad sat on a rooftop and looked out over London, the toxic city so filled with potential. For the first time ever in her new life, she was afraid.

CHAPTER SIX
FLEETER

As the Jeep slewed across the road and mounted the pavement, Jack grabbed Sparky's and Jenna's arms and pulled them backwards, just waiting for the next burst of gunfire.

Brakes squealed as the other two vehicles skidded to a halt. Someone shouted. Someone else screamed.

Jenna tripped and went down. Jack could have let her go, but he chose to hold on and fall with her. Sparky stood beside them, Jenna's knife suddenly in his hand.

The Jeep struck a building at the corner of the crossroads, and Jack cringed as he saw someone thrown through the already-shattered windscreen, blood spattering behind them. They slid across the crumpled bonnet and came to rest against the wall, motionless.

"Too late to run," Jack said. Something passed across his field of vision and he blinked rapidly.

The crashed Jeep's rear doors opened and three Choppers jumped out, guns at the ready, eyes wide and alert.

Jack searched inside. He delved into that sparkling constellation of potential Nomad had seeded within him, looking desperately for something that might help them. He grasped one idea he had used already and made the weapons hot, but the Choppers wore heavy gloves. He threw an image at one of them that they were breathing insects. Perhaps it was the Choppers' fear, or his own panic, but it was ineffective.

As Jack stood and helped Jenna to her feet, the three Choppers rushed forward and aimed their guns.

"Don't move!" one of them said, his voice incredibly high. There was blood splashed on his face.

"Just shoot them!" a second soldier said. Her head flipped back and her throat opened from ear to ear, her only scream a bubbling cry.

"Stop it!" the first soldier said. His gun was shaking as he aimed at Sparky, his comrade bleeding out on the ground beside him.

Something moved again. A blur, a smudge on reality. Jack blinked.

The soldier's gun vanished from his hands and then appeared again, barrel pressed against his forehead, held by a tall, stocky woman in a short dress.

"Where the hell did she come from?" Jenna asked.

"Out of thin air," Sparky said. "Let's hope she's on our side, eh?"

"Drop it!" the woman said, but the third soldier spun, bringing his own weapon to bear on the newly arrived woman.

She grinned, flitted out of view again, and the third soldier's head snapped back before the gunshot even sounded.

"Shit," Jenna said, turning away.

The other two Jeeps' doors sprung open and Choppers emerged, a dozen of them fanning out around their vehicles and quickly closing on the scene of slaughter.

"Shift!" Sparky said needlessly, and he grabbed Jenna's hand as the three of them darted for cover.

But Jack was watching, trying to perceive what was happening, and at the same time a particular star began to shine in his mind's eye. *There she is*, he thought, flooded with certainty that he would be able to follow the woman in the dress.

The last survivor from the crashed Jeep was pulling his sidearm, eyes on Jack, hatred on his face.

The woman had not reappeared, but from behind the vehicle came a startled cry, and then several guns started firing at once.

Sparky and Jenna reached a shop doorway and slid across the pavement until they were protected from the field of fire.

Jack breathed deeply. When Sparky turned to look at him, he smiled.

"J—!" Sparky shouted, and Jack let the power flood through him, scorching his veins, setting every nerve on fire with the thrilling potential of something he had never done before.

The world ground to a halt.

Jack caught his breath as every sense retreated to nothing. Sounds faded until all he heard was his own beating heart, and blood pulsing through his ears. The air was motionless. Smoke hung like Christmas decorations above the crashed Jeep's front end. Blood dripped from the dead soldier on its bonnet, each drop barely moving, exclamations on the air.

Sparky reached for Jack, mouth hanging open and bearing his unuttered name. Jenna was suspended halfway through a fall to the ground, hair streaming behind her, hand held out to arrest the impact, her eyes on Sparky.

Jack looked around at the Choppers, all similarly frozen—

But not *quite*. "Not quite still," Jack said. His voice did not echo, as if he'd spoken in an insulated chamber rather than in this bloodied London street. The Chopper pulling a gun on him *was* shifting slightly, his shoulder raising, hand tugging the pistol from its holster, movements as imperceptible as a minute hand on a clock. And Sparky's mouth opened wider, wider, as he shouted his friend's name in terror.

"Oh!" a surprised voice said. "Well. I thought I was the only one."

The woman in the dress appeared from behind the crashed Jeep and strolled casually across to the standing soldier. She stepped over one of the bodies without looking down, though Jack had seen her shoot the terrified man in the face.

"Who . . . ?" Jack said.

"Name's Fleeter," she said. She watched Jack curiously as she moved the soldier's hand aside and pulled the pistol from his belt. Then she smiled, and it made her look manic. "I wasn't told you could do this." She stepped back and aimed the gun at the man's head.

"Wait!" Jack said, his word cut off by the gunshot.

"Why?" the woman asked, all innocence. As she walked towards Jack, he saw the most terrible thing.

The bullet struck the Chopper's face in slow motion. It impacted his skin, entered just below his left eye socket, and sent a ripple of imminent destruction through the man's face.

Jack turned away, not wishing to see any more.

"So," the woman said, circling Jack so that she could see his face. "You want to help me with the rest of them?"

"No!" Jack said. "Who are you? *What* are you?"

"Reaper sent me to keep an eye on you. Make sure you didn't get into trouble."

She had already turned and was walking towards the other soldiers, her wide hips swaying the short skirt. She wasn't pretty, but she was striking. In Jack's eyes right now she was also monstrous, and he was desperate to prevent her continuing the slaughter.

Whatever these Choppers might do, they were still people, each with families and individual stories to tell.

"Why would he worry about me?"

The woman who had called herself Fleeter shrugged. "I just do as he tells me."

"Just following orders, eh? That's what these Choppers do. Hey. Hey!" She was approaching more of the soldiers and raising the stolen pistol.

Fleeter turned and looked over her shoulder, eyebrows raised in surprise. "What?"

"Don't," Jack said.

She pulled the trigger. The sound was a crushing impact and then an extended, deafening roar, like a train bursting from a tunnel and then receding. He saw the bullet leave the gun and strike a woman in the eye.

"*Don't!*" he shouted. He ran at Fleeter and she stepped aside, tripping him up. As Jack struck the ground his anger grew, and the pain from knees and elbows fed it. He delved deep and stood again, turning to the woman, sending a thought, spasming her thigh muscles so that she groaned and stumbled, dropping the gun and hitting the road.

"I said don't," Jack said. The gunshot's roar was a grumbling echo, fading, fading. "Now you can help me get my friends away from here."

"Can't," Fleeter said through gritted teeth.

"Why not?"

"I don't move people. I just speed myself up." She looked up at him, still trying to massage the cramps from her muscles. "Like you."

"You're nothing like me," Jack said. As he went to Sparky and Jenna he could feel the flow of time all around, moving like random currents in thick soup. *I'll carry them*, he thought. *Away from danger, hide somewhere, and then—*

Something slipped. Everything fluttered and blinked, and then noise and chaos burst around him—gunshots, shouting, someone screaming one name over and over again: "Peter! Peter! Peter!"

"—ack!" Sparky finished shouting, and his eyes went wide.

"What the bloody hell?" Jenna asked. "How did you get from there to—?"

Jack fell into the doorway with them, overcome with sensory input after that brief respite. Everything felt wrong—the air, the noise, the feel of concrete pavement against his hands. He looked around quickly for Fleeter, but saw only the crashed Jeep and the Choppers now advancing quickly from behind it.

"They'll kill us," Jack said, because it was inevitable. They'd seen their comrades ambushed and murdered, and here were the kids they'd likely been looking for all across London. Shoot now, ask questions later.

The Choppers fell one after another, legs kicked from beneath them. They hit the ground hard as if shoved from above by a massive weight. Bones broke.

With a clap of displaced air, Fleeter appeared before them. She looked angry.

"Well, come on then," she said. "Or I *will* have to finish them off." She limped along the street without looking back, and Jack grabbed his friends' hands.

"Come on!" he said, ignoring their questioning looks. "No time to lose." He and his friends followed the woman along the street.

Moments later the shooting began. Bullets ripped into parked cars and across storefronts, ricochets sparking from the road, and Fleeter led them between two buildings, protected from the shooting but nowhere near safe. She skidded to a halt and looked back, angry.

"You'll get me killed!" she said to Jack, and her fear was obvious. Desperate to use her ability to flit away, she had also been tasked with protecting Jack. *By my father*, Jack thought. But now was not the time to dwell on what that might mean.

"If you'll trust me, we'll be safe," Jack said.

They heard cautious footsteps and whispered orders, the crackling of radios, and in moments the Choppers would storm the alley. There would be no demands to raise hands, give in, kneel down. Only bullets.

"Safe here?" Fleeter said, gesturing around at the alley.

"There," Jack said. He pointed at a door alcove, where two red-painted fire doors were locked shut.

"Yeah," Sparky said. Jack could have hugged his friend for remembering, and Sparky's confidence seemed to change something in Fleeter.

"You can do other stuff," she said, surprised.

Sparky and Jenna were already in the alcove, squatting, nowhere near out of sight but ready for Jack to save them. He joined his friends there, already floating through his cosmos of fledgling abilities, reaching for one blazing star he already knew.

"They're brothers and fathers, daughters and mothers," he said softly. Fleeter seemed to vibrate, shimmering as though seen through a heavy heat-haze as she struggled with doubt—disappear into her own slowed-down time and continue with her cold-blooded slaughter; or trust Jack?

As Jack held his friends' hands and breathed deeply, Fleeter joined them, pressing one warm hand to the back of his neck. It was sticky with blood, and when she whispered to him, her voice was heavy with the threat of more.

"This goes wrong, I'll only save myself," she said.

"Clear!" a voice shouted, and Jack and the others turned slowly to look along the alley.

Two Choppers stood just beyond the entrance, one crouched down and aiming a machine gun, the other peering around the wall. *We're in plain sight but a world away*, Jack thought. The woman with the machine gun swung the weapon back and forth to cover the alley, its barrel drifting past the alcove where they squatted and back again. The barrel did not waver.

"Okay, quick and careful," a voice said. Two more Choppers entered the alley and started moving along, guns always at the ready. Jack saw their wide, scared eyes. He could almost smell their fear.

Sparky and Jenna both squeezed his hands at the same time, and he squeezed back. He felt Fleeter's blood-sticky hand resting on the back of his neck, and close to his ear she breathed a quick, sharp laugh.

We're not here, he thought, *the alcove is empty, no one hiding here, red doors, red doors . . .*

The Choppers passed them, one stepping a foot away from Jenna's right leg. Jack knew that though he could convince the soldiers that the alcove was empty, if they stepped on one of them, the game was over.

He tried not to think too much about what he was doing. He was aware that he was shaking—and that his friends were holding his hands tightly, unable to help but keen to show they were there—and he could feel the immensity of the power he was tapping into. In his mind's eye he orbited the giant star of this ability, drawing dregs away for himself and all the while wondering what would happen if he plummeted inside.

"Wait!" a Chopper shouted, and Jack swayed where he knelt, his vision clearing, expecting to see a machine-gun barrel swinging his way and lining up on his face.

Something yowled along the alley and a shape scampered up a wall, leaping from sill to sill, back and forth across the alley as it gained height.

"Bloody cat!" a woman's voice said. "Scared the crap out of me, almost shot—"

"Quiet!" someone hissed. "They might be nearby."

The Choppers advanced, leaving two of their number at the alley's entrance facing outward. Their fear was obvious, and Jack tried to put himself in their shoes—hunting strange people with powers they could not understand, and some of whom only wanted every Chopper dead. It was a war like no other. But Jack could not stretch to feeling sorry for them. Not after everything he'd heard about what they did.

And not now that they had his mother and sister.

He glanced up and back at Fleeter, and in her eyes he saw a glimpse of what he had been feeling. She looked down at him and raised her eyebrows. But he shook his head and relaxed down again, concentrating, knowing that soon they would be able to get away.

Murder could not be the answer. The more fighting and deaths, the harder it would be to set aside arms and rein in powers when the time came. The fighting had begun because people had changed, and it would only stop if everyone was able to change some more.

They waited there for ten more minutes, until the Choppers realised that they'd lost their quarry and ran back along the alley. The soldiers bickered and swore at each other, and a couple of them laughed. Jack knew they were venting, and perhaps also relieved that they'd lost their targets. Their comrades lying dead back at the crossroads were testament to what another contact might bring.

Fleeter moved away from Jack, and as he relaxed and breathed himself back to normal, she disappeared in a blur, air smashing in to fill the void where she had been standing.

"Who the hell is she?" Sparky asked.

"Fleeter. Reaper sent her to watch over us."

"Your father?" Jenna said. "Why?"

Jack shrugged. "Don't know. She might be watching us now, though. She can take herself out of phase with everyone else. Speed up, so that everything's slowed down. She'll be to the end of the street and back again while we can blink."

"And now you can do it too," Sparky said.

"Yeah." Jack nodded, looked at his friends, and released their hands. They did not comment or back away, but he could still sense that strange distance between them. It made him incredibly sad.

"So what's it like?" Sparky asked. Jack was so grateful to his friend for even asking, but before he could respond Fleeter was back. With a *clap!* she appeared before them, litter and dust swirling from the displaced air.

"They're gathering their dead and leaving," she said. She was a stern woman, her features seemingly sculpted rather than grown, and Jack could not help wondering who and what she had been. The short dress seemed incongruous on this woman; this killer.

"So now what?" Jenna asked.

Fleeter raised her eyebrows, looking at Jenna and Sparky properly for the first time. Then she stared at Jack again, and he could see confusion bubbling beneath her outward confidence.

"Now you take me to Reaper," Jack said.

"What?" Fleeter said.

"Reaper. My father. You take us to him." Jack stood, remaining close to his friends. "I'm sure he'll want to see me. He sent you to watch over me, after all."

Fleeter started glancing away, as if unable to hold Jack's gaze. *She's scared of me*, he thought. And though that idea did not sit comfortably with him—he had no desire to instil fear in anyone—he also knew that it might help.

"Thanks for saving us," Jenna said. "They'd have probably killed us and taken Jack."

"Probably," Fleeter said. "He's special. You're not."

"Everyone's special," Jenna said.

"I'm not," Sparky said, trying to joke. But no one smiled.

"We've seen horrible things since we came into the city," Jenna went on. "The stuff the Choppers do to Irregulars, and sometimes people like you. People who call themselves Superior. And we've seen what you do to the Choppers, too."

"They deserve it!" Fleeter said.

"After what they did to my father, I shouldn't argue," Jenna said. She nodded at Fleeter's questioning glance. "This reaches way beyond what's left of London."

"I don't care about anything beyond," Fleeter said. "That no longer exists." She moved away from them all slightly, standing close to the alley entrance and leaning to look out along the street.

"Then you're blinkered and stupid," Jenna said. "You must know this can't all go on forever."

"The more they send, the more we kill," Fleeter said.

"And what about the illness killing people even now?" Jenna asked.

"We'll find a cure."

"No," Jenna said. "There won't be a cure. Not from in here, at least. What were you? A solicitor? A reporter? Checkout girl?"

"What I was before doesn't matter."

"Of *course* it does!" Jenna said. "You might be able to skip here and there without anyone seeing, and . . . and slit people's throats before them even knowing. But you're no doctor or scientist. No one will cure what's killing people like you until London is exposed, and outside help comes in."

"People like me?" Fleeter asked, and for a moment she seemed furious. But then she calmed as quickly as she had become enraged, and looked down at her feet.

"Are you sick?" Jenna asked softly.

"No. Not yet. But . . ."

"But?" Jack asked.

"There are those amongst the Superiors who believe it's a blight introduced by Miller and his people. To kill us all. Finally turn London toxic for good."

"It wouldn't surprise me," Jack said. They all remained silent for a while, and in the distance they heard motors retreating into the city.

"No," Jenna said. "No surprise at all. But it's dooming something wonderful to an early end."

"Reaper won't let it happen," Fleeter said.

"Reaper used to be my father," Jack said. "He worked in an office, liked banana sandwiches, watched motor-racing on a Sunday afternoon. He went running lots, and my mother never really understood that. He said it was a better mid-life crisis than having an affair. He collected *Star Wars* figures. Didn't like milk in his coffee. I saw him crying once when we were watching *ET*."

Fleeter went to speak, but said nothing. She shook her head.

"Reaper can't save you all," Jack said. "But I'm beginning to think I can. Now take us to him."

Fleeter turned her back on them. For a moment Jack thought she was going to wink out of existence again and leave them all behind, and he knew he would not follow. But then she walked slowly, cautiously out into the street.

Jack and his friends started to follow.

CHAPTER SEVEN
BLACKBERRIES

"**S**he was there. She was *there!*"

"I didn't see anyone," Rook said.

"There, in that open doorway, watching me!" Lucy-Anne pointed at the building she had only ducked into before realising it was empty and lifeless. She had not been afraid to continue inside, but she had been certain that to do so would be pointless. The woman was already gone.

"Nomad," Lucy-Anne said. "That's who she is. The wanderer. The ghost of London."

"Nomad's a myth," Rook said.

"And what do you think you are to everyone outside?"

Rook looked troubled. He glanced between Lucy-Anne and the empty building, and she could see that he believed what he said—he'd seen no one there, and to him, Nomad *was* a myth.

"We should get going," he said. "Dusk soon. Good time to get into the north."

"There's a boundary?" Lucy-Anne asked.

"Only in your head." Rook set off and Lucy-Anne followed, but she paused to glance back several times at the open doorway. The place had once been a hotel, and she wondered how many rooms with closed doors still housed the rotten remains of the dead.

Amongst them had walked Nomad, seeking a place from which she could observe Lucy-Anne.

She's there in my dreams, and now I'm seeing her for real.

Rook took them through the back end of London—hidden places, alleys and areas that only people who knew they were there would be able to find. Some of them wound behind rows of houses, paths overgrown with rose bushes gone wild and clematis given free rein now that there was no-one there to trim it. Other narrow, cobbled roads seemed to be left over from a much older London emerged from hiding, and if it weren't for the dusty vehicles sitting on flattened tyres, Lucy-Anne might have believed they had gone back in time.

In some places there were bodies. Shrivelled, dried remnants, or gnawed bones scattered by carrion creatures. Lucy-Anne was surprised how quickly the shock faded.

Dusk settled quickly across these hidden places. Shadows seemed to stretch out from where they had been resting during the day, washing across the ground, climbing walls, enveloping everything and striving to hide things from view. Lucy-Anne felt safe with Rook, and she could still see and sometimes hear his birds following them above, or flitting from roof to roof around them. But that did not prevent her from being unsettled as night approached.

Going north made the darkness deeper.

As Rook led the way, Lucy-Anne noticed something of a change come over him. At first she thought perhaps it was the failing light that seemed to bleed some of his confidence. But he moved slower, more cautiously, until he stopped at the end of an alleyway leading out onto a wide shopping street. He stood facing away from her with his arm held out, and a rook shadowed down and landed on his upturned wrist.

The bird was silent, head jerking left and right and looking everywhere but at Rook.

"What is it?" Lucy-Anne asked.

"I'm afraid," Rook said. As he spoke the bird gave a *caw-caw!* and flapped its wings, but remained perched on his arm. Perhaps it was afraid as well.

The admission shocked Lucy-Anne. After she'd seen Rook in action with Reaper she'd viewed him in the same way. Despite his protestations, she saw him as a Superior, a person who considered themselves as more than human, and better.

"Afraid?" she asked.

"I can be, you know," he said.

"I know, but . . ."

"Can't you sense it?" he asked, turning around to face her. The bird watched her, dark eyes inscrutable.

She tried to feel what he was feeling, sniffing the air, listening for anything out of the ordinary, and then closing her eyes. But she felt only what she had ever since entering London—dislocation, and an idea that she could never belong here at all.

"It's *wild*!" Rook said. He was speaking quietly, glancing about as he did so. Afraid of being watched. "I've only ever been this far north once before, and I turned back and ran. Got lost south of the river, and it felt like going home. Back to my mother's womb. Safe."

"What's so terrible about it?"

"London changed, but this part changed more than anywhere. It's a different place now. Those left behind here don't even pretend to be what they were before."

"And everyone else does?" she asked doubtfully.

"Even Reaper admits to being human."

She glanced past him into the deserted street, lit only by the faint glow of dusk and the rising moon. "Then what about people here?"

"Like I said. Wild. Just . . ." He reached out and touched her, and it was like a feather across her cheek. "Just be warned."

"But you'll protect me," she said. "You know how."

"I know how to try."

"I have no choice," Lucy-Anne said. "My brother's out there somewhere. That's all I am now. Searching for him defines me."

Rook nodded once, then glanced away. "Follow me," he said. "We'll cut across the street, then through some gardens. Then there's a wide road, and we're in Regent's Park."

"And why are we going there?"

"It'll probably be quicker passing through the park than along streets."

"And safer?"

"Didn't say that."

The enormity of their task, always at the back of Lucy-Anne's mind, came to the fore then. Andrew was a needle in a haystack, a pebble on a beach. And now that they were heading into the wilder north of London, the haystack and beach were more dangerous than ever.

There were six corpses propped against the wall at the edge of the park. Each had a small fire lit in its lap, their arms had been interlocked in a grotesque mockery of dancing, and their heads and shoulders were encased in silvery-grey webbing. They were naked apart from their shoes. That's what Lucy-Anne noticed first, before the rest of the horror. That they all wore shoes.

"What's this?" she whispered. Rook squatted beside her in the shelter of a bus stop, two of his birds on the ground beside him. A third bird drifted in through the dark and settled on his shoulder, and he tilted his head.

"Don't know," he said, answering her at last. "There'll be plenty we can't explain. But the coast is clear." He went to stand, and Lucy-Anne grabbed his arm.

"Clear?" she asked. She did not want to see the bodies, yet that was the only thing she could look at. She wondered if they were Choppers. "Clear?"

"So my birds tell me," Rook said. "And I trust them. Come on."

They crossed diagonally across the street, moving away from the bodies with the fires in their laps and towards the hulking shadow of an open park gate. If they were a warning, Lucy-Anne's every atom told her to take heed. But her mind drove her on towards Andrew.

The smell of burning flesh accompanied them into the park, and she wondered how often this warning was replaced. And as she and Rook passed through the wide gates and onto the first of the curving footpaths, she froze in shock.

Empty, dead London was an unnatural place. Once home to endless bustle, with streets awash with life and millions of separate stories every day, and squares echoing to birdsong and the lilts of a hundred languages, the new silence of the toxic city was alien and unnatural. Before she left for good, Lucy-Anne had once remained behind in school on a dare, hiding until the caretakers locked her in, emerging into darkness, prowling the corridors and classrooms with every intention of performing small acts of rebellion and graffiti. But she had found the place so disconcerting—silence where once was life; breathlessness where echoes should live—that she'd smashed a window to escape.

London felt like that now.

But the park was worse.

They didn't have to go too far in before they heard the calls and hoots, the whistles and moans. It sounded like Lucy-Anne imagined a jungle would sound at night, except . . . different. There was an intelligence to some of these calls that sent a shiver down her spine. Strange smells assailed her nostrils, and when she tried breathing through her mouth she tasted something acidic and damp on the air.

In the weak moonlight, shadows danced beneath trees seemingly in defiance of the motionless canopies. Wide swathes of lawn had grown into seas of long grasses. Things moved in there.

The sheer wilderness of the place was overwhelming, and Lucy-Anne kept close to Rook.

"Can't we go around?" she whispered.

"You saw what awaited us out there," he said. "We're in the north now. The streets around here . . ." He shrugged but said no more.

"You've sent your rooks to see?" she asked. Rook did not reply. He seemed unsettled, tense, so she did not force the issue. Her one desire became to make it through the park and out the other side.

The path they followed soon vanished beneath a spread of tough grass, and Rook grabbed her hand and pulled her towards a wall of darkness beneath a copse of trees. Lucy-Anne did not want to go that way—she felt like a child afraid of the dark—but Rook's birds swooped in and away again, one landing on his shoulder as soon as another took off. She could only assume that they were imparting information and telling him whether it was safe. Her life was in his hands.

She had not willingly been totally dependent on another person for a very long time.

As they approached the trees Lucy-Anne saw the first shadow moving down amongst the boles. It darted from tree to tree through the shadows, seemingly merging with one trunk before skitting across to the next.

Calls and cries came from across the park, but the copse before them had fallen silent.

Rook paused, head on one side and a rook *caw*ing on his shoulder. "You'll see strange things," he said, then he walked on.

Lucy-Anne took a deep breath and followed. Something caressed her ear and she waved at it, expecting to find a drooping branch. But she touched nothing, and when she glanced up she saw a shadow lifting and dipping above her as it flapped its strong, silent wings. Other rooks hovered farther away. Protecting her.

The shape slinked out from behind the first of the trees, scampering through the grass and then standing upright on two legs to glare at them. It was a man, but his arms and legs were deformed and bent like a dog's. At first she thought he was black, but then she spotted the pale patches of skin across his stomach and abdomen, and realised that he was mostly covered in a heavy, dark pelt. His face protruded, nose wide, wet nostrils opening and closing as he took in their scents.

He shouted at them, and it was a bark. It sounded pained.

"Don't panic," Rook said.

"Oh my God," Lucy-Anne said, appealing to a deity she had forgotten since her childhood. "Oh my God, what is that, what *is* that?"

"A man turning into a dog," Rook said.

Lucy-Anne laughed out loud at his stark answer. But he was right.

The man shouted again, a heavy, deep bark that could not have issued from a human's throat. He fell to all fours again and scampered away, kicking through the long grass, skitting back and forth, and a rudimentary tail swished the air behind him. Soon he was lost to the darkness, and moonlight could touch him no more.

Lucy-Anne was glad. She wished the moon and stars would shut themselves away for the rest of the night.

Amongst the trees, the darkness was even deeper. Rook moved quickly, and every now and then one of his birds would flit down out of the darkness and land on his shoulder. They were scouting the way forward, but Lucy-Anne knew that they might not see everything. There could be anything hiding in the dark.

A man turning into a dog! she thought. She had never seen or imagined anything like it, and it was a whole new aspect to what had happened to London. She'd heard of and met people whom

Doomsday had changed, giving them talents or abilities that had been pure science fiction until two years ago. But the changes had all been on the inside. Here, things were different.

"Rook, what is this?" she whispered. He kept walking. "Rook?"

He paused and turned around. "We need to move quickly," he said. And that was all. Any explanation would have to wait until later, because he set off again at a fast pace. Sometimes, Lucy-Anne had to run to keep up.

They passed through the wooded area, and just as they emerged close to a lake several shadows rose from the ground before them. Rook skidded to a halt, startled, and Lucy-Anne bumped into him. She maintained the contact.

Rooks flapped and cawed somewhere out of sight.

The shapes were people, naked, caked in mud, hair set in extravagant designs. Their limbs seemed too short, too thin. When they moved, Lucy-Anne saw why.

They had reared up from their stomachs, and the first woman slumped down to the ground and curled away through the undergrowth. She shifted from side to side as she went, withered, sore-covered arms dragging along on either side and legs fused along their insides to form a long, thin tail.

As Lucy-Anne gasped, the woman hissed. The two other snake-people eased back down onto their stomachs and followed the woman, and soon they were lost from view.

"They were . . ." Lucy-Anne said.

"Lucky we surprised them," Rook said. "Let's hurry before they come back."

"Are they poisonous? Constrictors? Do they . . . how much like real snakes *are* they?"

"You want to stay and find out?" He ran and she followed him, skirting around the lake's edge but not getting too close. Things were splashing in there. From the dark came wretched cries. *It must hurt them*, she thought. *Such a huge change, so quickly. It must* hurt! Though scared of them, she also felt pity.

Rook ran over a small footbridge that passed over a stream leading into the lake, and without pause headed across a wide area of long-grassed lawn spotted with occasional clumps of trees and wooden seating shelters. Moonlight silvered the land, setting fire to treetops. To their left and right shadows ran to keep pace with them, but Lucy-Anne could only assume that Rook knew about them. A rook landed on her left shoulder, its surprising lightness startling her, and a thought came unbidden: *They're graceful and beautiful*. She understood some of Rook's attachment to these creatures then, and for the first time she felt a pang of jealousy at his incredible abilities. Perhaps because he was closer to them than he ever could be to her.

They approached another small wooded area. She wondered why Rook was leading them into the trees instead of around them, and then she saw the shadowy humps across the grassland to their right. They moved slowly, sluggishly, but they seemed to be much larger than normal people. She was so glad that darkness mostly hid them from view.

"What the hell?" she asked, but he did not answer. He was focussed, committed to getting them across the park safely, past the mutations and the dangers, and she had to wonder why. He was not the heartless boy she had assumed when they had met. If anything he was confused and conflicted, hiding behind his grief over his dead mother and brother, sheltering emotions with his unusual abilities and the deadly opportunities they afforded him. Perhaps being with her was the first chance he'd had to properly express himself in two years.

They entered the wooded area, and as she opened her mouth to call him to a stop, to hold him and thank him, a shocking sense settled over Lucy-Anne that she had been to this place before.

With my parents, my brother, on one of those days we came to London?
Surely I wouldn't recognise it still, especially in the dark and with how much
things have changed? Maybe I saw pictures? Maybe it's a famous view of
Regent's Park that's used for—

And then she smelled blackberries.

It was her dream. And soon would come the park bench smothered by shrubs, and then the monkey-man swinging down from the trees at her, and then the ground would open up to swallow Rook, and she would look down into the hole to see—

"Rook!" she shouted, and he skidded to a halt before her. The sense of déjà vu was still all-encompassing, and she tried to break it. If she could move on from the conviction that this had all happened before, maybe she could change things. *Not every dream comes true*, she thought. *Rook and me in the house, making love . . . that hasn't happened, yet.* And she stepped forward and reached for Rook, grasping his jacket and pulling him close, ignoring his startled expression and pressing her lips to his. He was unresponsive and cold, and he shoved her away.

"No," she said, "no, don't. Just . . . thank you. For doing this. But . . ." She looked around. There was no bench, and no man swinging down at her from the trees. She sighed, and it shook her whole body.

"What?" Rook asked. He took her hands in his and waited until she looked up at him. "What is it?"

"Blackberries," she said. "I smell them."

"Not in season."

She took in a breath and smelled damp soil, rain, and the warm tang of evergreens.

"No," she said. "You're right. Not blackberries at all."

Frowning, he grasped her right hand tight and tugged her on. The first few steps were painful because she expected the ground to open at any minute and for them to tumble into the pit. But when that did not happen, and they emerged close to the northern edge of the park, she started running more freely. She experienced a moment of utter delight and well-being, and when they reached the boundary wall she grabbed Rook again and kissed him properly. This time he relaxed slightly into her embrace, but his eyes remained open and alert.

A rook landed on his shoulder and stared at her quizzically.

Lucy-Anne laughed. There was a hint of hysteria to the sound, and Rook looked as befuddled as his bird.

"It's okay," she said. "It's fine."

"Well, we're through the park, at least," he said. "Come on. Long way to go."

In the streets, that feeling of well-being left her as quickly as it had come. When the first piercing shriek rang out, and was taken up by many others, Lucy-Anne wondered whether they had actually avoided anything at all.

CHAPTER EIGHT
THE NEW

A s they walked through the twilit streets of a changed, ruined London, Jack started to experiment with the universe of possibilities he had been given. Each time he probed in towards the sparks of potential inside he tasted Nomad's finger on his tongue. It was an exotic, scary taste, and he thought perhaps he might become addicted.

Fleeter led the way, incongruous with her blood-spattered hands and party dress. Sparky and Jenna followed her, walking close together. Jack brought up the rear. He had not asked Fleeter where they were going. He and his friends were exhausted—since entering London they had been pushed from one trial to another, with barely any time to rest—and he craved some peace. If Fleeter kept her words to take them to Reaper, perhaps they would find some.

Or maybe everything would get worse.

They were walking along a narrow residential street. Dark windows observed their progress, and Jack grasped a spark, letting it seed in his mind and grow into something amazing. He probed towards one house and felt his way inside, tasting the happiness that had once dwelled there. He heard children laughing, adults loving, a dog barking as it played with a young boy, and the chiming of a music box in a little girl's pink room. He smiled . . . but then felt suddenly queasy when the reality of that house now hit home. The parents sat dead and decomposed in the living room, and the children were not there at all. The family had died apart.

Wiping tears from his eyes, Jack snatched at something else.

His fingers tingled. Sparks jumped beneath his fingernails, lightening his quicks and shadowing the bones of his hands against red flesh. He touched one of the cars still parked neatly along the kerb, and the sizzle of electricity snapped at the metal chassis, cracking the windscreen and drawing smoke from the half-flat tyres.

Sparky and Jenna jumped and span around, eyes wide. Seeing what he was doing did nothing to lessen their shock. Lightning danced across the car's roof and bonnet, and illuminated the dank insides.

"Come on," Fleeter said, feigning boredom. But he saw the interest even in her eyes.

Jack snapped his fingers and sparks jumped from them, fading in the air around his head. Sparky and Jenna were watching, and he smiled. They smiled back, but their uncertainty was clear.

As they walked, he tried to dip in to other abilities. Sometimes it worked, sometimes not. He heard his friends' heartbeats from a dozen paces away, but when he tried to lure a kestrel down from above the bird ignored him. He sensed an Irregular watching them from behind a dusty window, felt the woman's sadness and fear, and he could almost taste the sickness settling upon her. But when he attempted to grasp the star that might enable him to communicate with her—to tell her, without speaking, that he promised to do what he could to help—he failed. Feedback squealed in his own mind, voice distorted and pained.

Uncertainties haunted him. Incredible powers were his, but so too was doubt, and a fear that when the time came to access these powers to save his friends, or himself, he would fail. The vast scope of potential within him was growing, but perhaps he could not move fast enough to keep up.

Jack jogged past his friends until he walked level with Fleeter.

"So where are we going?" he asked.

"To Reaper, just as you asked."

"You're sure? You're not taking us somewhere else, like . . . a trap. Trick us, lock us away for a while?"

"You don't trust me?" she asked.

Jack said nothing. He wasn't sure of the answer.

Fleeter chuckled. "You'd just pick the lock anyway. Or melt it, snap it, or make it not there."

"I don't know," he said.

"I've never seen anyone like you," she said, but she trailed off, moving quickly ahead.

"But you've heard about someone like me," he said. "Nomad."

Fleeter gave no sign that she'd heard. At the road junction she turned left, then cut a quick right through an alleyway.

"Where are we going?" Jack asked again.

"Trust me," Fleeter said.

"I don't trust her as far as I could throw her," Sparky said aloud, and Jenna laughed.

"I don't think you'd ever get close enough to try."

"You two okay?" Jack asked.

"Yeah," Jenna said.

"Dandy," Sparky said.

Jack nodded. He felt the weight of responsibility upon him—it would be down to him to talk to Reaper, persuade him of their cause, convince him not to simply abandon them, or worse. But having his friends with him meant the world.

Changing, he needed them now more than ever.

He wondered what his mother and Emily were doing right now. He tried to imagine them safe and sound, perhaps locked in the same room in Camp H. They would support each other, and Emily would likely be lively and chirpy, singing songs and insisting that her mother sing along.

All the while, though, a different image played behind that one. The more he tried to ignore it—the metal bed, dissection equipment, gutters running with blood—the clearer it became.

He searched for a star that might show him his family, but found none.

"Damn it," Jack said, shaking his head and fighting the tears. But the more he fought, the more insistent they became. "Damn it!"

"Jack?" Jenna said.

"We don't have much time," he said. "Fleeter. Hey. How soon?"

She glanced back over her shoulder. "Almost there."

"Almost where?" Sparky asked.

"Almost . . ." she said, trailing off, walking on.

Jack's friends comforted him, but neither asked what he had seen or sensed to bring on his tears. He wished they had. He wanted to tell them that it was nothing but a normal, very human fear for his loved ones.

Fleeter paused with her hand held up and then vanished with a *clap!* that echoed from surrounding buildings, leaving them abandoned and alone.

Jack started pacing, but Jenna urged him to remain calm, convincing both Jack and Sparky that the woman would be back. "Why lead us all this way just to disappear?" she asked.

"Trap?" Sparky suggested.

Jack tried to search around them, sense out danger, but his heart was too hurried. He could not concentrate. And when Fleeter appeared before them again, he slumped against Sparky and sighed with relief.

"Choppers," she said. "Come on."

"What did you do to them?" Jack asked.

"Slowed them down." Fleeter grinned. "Punctures. They'll be

going home tonight to see their loved ones, don't you worry, Jack."
Loaded with sarcasm the words might have been, still they came as
a relief. Jack had seen far too many people die already, and he would
do everything he could from now on to prevent any more.

They passed an old indoor market, grand architecture crumbled
and ignored long before Doomsday, and Jack became more alert. Something about the way Fleeter moved told him that something was going
to happen soon. She looked back more often, smiling uncertainly.

"Fleeter, please tell me that—" he began, but then she was gone
again.

"Damn it!" he shouted. Pigeons took flight from atop the
market building, and somewhere in the far distance a scream
sounded, rising high and then quickly cut off. Jack's wasn't the only
drama being played out in London this evening. But it was probably
the most important.

"She'll be back," Jenna said.

"You think?" Sparky said. "Spooks the chit out of me, that one."

"She's brought us this far," Jenna said.

"How far? She's dumped us outside this old place, and what the
hell happens now? D'you know where we are?"

"Not really," Jenna admitted quietly.

"Jack?" Sparky asked.

"Well . . ."

"You could do a Superman to find out, I suppose," Sparky said.
He was becoming agitated, stepping from foot to foot. "But what
good's any of that done us so far? Huh?"

Jack's mind was spinning. He searched inside for something to
help, some way to move them forward, but his confusion blurred
everything. He felt more useless than ever.

"I'll go on my own," he said. "You two leave. I've dragged you
here, too far, too dangerous. And really, it's—"

"You tell us it's nothing to do with us and I'll deck you," Sparky said, and right then Jack knew that he meant it.

Clap! Fleeter appeared across the street from them, swirling up a twisting cloud of dust and litter. She smoothed down her dress and ran a hand through her hair.

"What?" she asked. Then she smiled, knowing what she had done. "Come on. Reaper will see you."

"He's near?" Sparky asked.

"Well, quite near. Come on. Bit of crawling to do."

"Crawling?" Jack asked.

"S'pose we've done enough running, flying, and walking today," Sparky said.

Fleeter led them around the side of the large market building, and where a huge tangle of old stalls was piled in a rusting heap against one moss-covered brick wall, she went down on her knees.

Back beneath the ground, Jack thought. Breezer and his friends hid under the Choppers' noses, but it surprised Jack that his father would hide himself away.

Wary, alert for the first aggressive move from Fleeter, he was the first to follow her.

It was difficult to actually tell when they went below ground again. Through the tangle of market stalls, their route led past a tumble of bricks, down a short concrete slope, through a pile of timber slumped with damp, and then they dropped into a larger duct. Fleeter hefted a torch from her pocket. They could almost stand here, but not quite, and they followed Fleeter stooped over. Sparky cursed several times when he banged his head on the pipes and ducting trays above them, and by the time they reached a larger junction area, blood was dribbling down his face. Jenna tutted and dabbed at his scalp with the sleeve of her jacket, and Sparky raised an eyebrow at Jack.

He wants me to fix it, Jack thought. He delved inside and circled the star he thought might help. But there was no time right now, because Fleeter was stopping for nothing. He merely nodded at his friends and then carried on.

Jack tried to keep track of their route. If something went wrong down here—if it was a trap, or something worse—they might have to come back up quickly. But he quickly lost his way. Crawling, scrambling, and climbing on occasion, he tried to access an ability that might help him map their route in his mind. His senses expanded until he could sense water courses and pipes streaming around them, but they did not need water. He grasped another spark and heard a whisper of voices overlying each other, and quickly withdrew when he realised he was hearing Sparky remembering an argument between his parents and dead brother. He shook his head, feeling grubby, as if he had intruded on something personal. The more confused he became, the greater his anger at being unable to help them. Nomad had seeded an ocean of possibilities within him, but had never told him how to use them.

"I feel like a rat," Sparky said as they passed along a dry sewer.

"You smell like one," Jenna said.

"That's the sewer, I'll have you know."

"Nah. It's dried up. Old crap. The smell's you. You stink of *rat*."

"This way," Fleeter said from ahead, paying no attention.

They left the sewer through a hole in one wall and headed down an uneven slope. It reminded Jack inevitably of their journey into London through the hidden subterranean route, and he kept his ears open for wild dogs or anything else that might cause them problems. But Fleeter moved with a casual confidence, and he thought she had been this way many times before.

He sensed someone watching them. Hairs on his neck bristled and he looked back. In the wavering light he saw Jenna and Sparky also looking around them, their own natural senses piqued. They both looked at him. Expecting something of him. So Jack closed his eyes briefly, drifted through his cosmos of potential, and smiled when he found what he was looking for.

"Through there," he said, pointing at a gap in the wall none of them had noticed before. "Shade. That shadow guy we saw with Reaper before."

Fleeter glanced back at Jack, mildly surprised. She aimed her torch directly back at his face, and he turned away, dazzled.

"He's there to make sure no one gets in who shouldn't," she said.

"Or out," a voice said from the dark gap in the wall. A chuckle followed, and Jack tried not to show his fear.

"Cheery bastard," Sparky said. "Maybe the smell's coming from him."

"Sparky!" Jenna said.

But Fleeter only laughed. "Come on. Almost there."

They went through another tunnel and emerged into what seemed to be a natural cavern. Dead, dried roots hung from the ceiling, and a swathe of spiderwebs hazed the ceiling from view. Jack shivered. He'd never liked spiders, and he wondered what they ate down here.

"Oh, gross," Jenna said, and Jack saw where she was pointing. Several rat corpses hung directly above them, spun in silk yet still clearly visible.

"Reaper?" Fleeter asked.

"Yes," a deep voice said, and Jack recognised his father instantly. He had seen him kill with that voice; one word could shatter bones and boil blood. And try though he did, Jack could find nothing in it that reminded him of the man he had once loved. "Yes, thank you, Fleeter."

"I did say sorry," she said, voice rising slightly.

A sigh from somewhere in the cavern. Then silence.

"Shall I . . ." she asked.

"Yes," Reaper said. "Send them in."

She aimed her torch into the cavern's corner and looked at Jack, Sparky and Jenna. She nodded ahead. "Go on. Through."

Jack went first. As he passed through the crack in the wall he thought about what he was going to say to his father, and what Reaper might say back. He was nervous, but also excited. He'd seen *something* of the father he had once loved left in Reaper, he was sure of it, and now was the time to—

But in the place beyond the cavern, shock froze Jack motionless.

Reaper was standing just beyond the opening that had been melted through concrete and brick sometime in the past, and beyond him was a room from the past. Jack had seen places like this in old war movies his mother used to enjoy, peopled by thin-moustached soldiers and pretty uniformed women. They'd all spoken very properly. The men had smoked and looked worried, and the women had taken calls on old-fashioned phones and pushed small flags around a large table.

This room must have once been one of those old war rooms. High-ceilinged, one long wall had a platform halfway up, and a man Jack recognised stood there, leaning casually on a rickety-looking handrail. His name was Puppeteer, and he had almost killed Jack's little sister.

Past Reaper, the huge table in the centre of the room was taken with a map of London. Sheets of paper were taped together to form one continuous map, and at its edges were areas of splashed red paint. The red formed a boundary, and Jack assumed this represented the Exclusion Zone, that collar of firebombed and flattened suburbs now separating London from the rest of the world.

"I thought I told you to run," Reaper said.

"You did," Jack said. "And we did, just before you murdered Miller."

Reaper raised an eyebrow. It was a startlingly familiar expression, one that used to denote humour when his father was normal. But now it was something else. It spoke of superiority.

"Who said I murdered him?"

Jack let it go. It might have been a word game and he was too tired, and too afraid for his family, to indulge.

"What's this?" Jack asked. On the London map were perhaps two dozen small blue flags, reminiscent of the Choppers' uniform colour. There were other flags, too—red, yellow, white. What they were meant to represent was more obscure.

A tall, extremely thin black woman with startlingly white hair stood beside the table. Now and then she would reach out and touch a flag, pause, look to the ceiling, and then move it slightly across the map. Sometimes she touched a flag and then seemed to have second thoughts, shifting her spindly hand to another flag before moving it. Her arms were incredibly long. She blinked slowly at Jack, barely acknowledging his and his friends' presence.

"What does it look like?" Reaper said.

"A war room," Sparky said.

Reaper barely glanced at Sparky and Jenna before focussing on Jack again. They stood there in silence for a moment, cool subterranean breath wafting through the gap in the wall behind them. The stone and concrete had been melted and reset, and Jack wondered by what. A Superior, perhaps. But he would not ask.

"We need to talk," he said to Reaper, and the tall man's expression did not flicker.

"He followed me," Fleeter said. "Some Choppers found them, so I flipped and took them out . . . most of them, at least. And Jack followed me."

"He flipped too?" Reaper said. He could not hide his surprise, and in that unguarded moment Jack saw something of his father. Just a flash, but it was there.

"I told you," Jack said. "Nomad touched me. And *you* told *me* she didn't exist."

Reaper—his father—stared at him. Jack felt like a child examined by an adult, a mouse being scrutinised by a cat. But he did not flinch.

"I saw her once," Reaper said. "But I don't believe in her."

"Maybe you're scared that she's more powerful than you?"

Reaper was silent for a long time, never once taking his eyes from Jack. The stare was a challenge; Jack stood up to it. Then Reaper said, "Perhaps we do need to talk. Fleeter, feed his friends, and show them where they can rest." He looked up at Sparky and Jenna, his expression stern. "You're tired."

No backchat, Sparky, Jack thought. *Please, not now when we might be getting somewhere.*

But Jenna said, "Yeah," and Fleeter moved off to their left. Sparky and Jenna followed, and Sparky threw a glance back at Jack that said, *Gonna be okay?*

Jack smiled, nodded. Yes. He'd be okay.

"Where shall we talk, Dad?"

From the moment Reaper led him away from the war room, Jack felt a confidence that belied everything that had happened. Following the man who had been his father, he plunged into that tumultuous, ever-expanding universe of abilities and closed on one without even thinking, feeling its heat, sensing its incredible gravity. He smiled as it filled his consciousness, and he was suddenly awash in a sea of beautiful memories. These times with his family warmed and calmed him, and made him feel that everything really was going to be all right.

But they were not for him.

That's the first time I've used it without real effort, he thought. Nomad's scent touched his nostrils, her taste flooded his mouth. It was something amazing.

This was certainly no James Bond–style secret base. The subterranean rooms must have been flooded in the past, and a layer of moss covered the walls up to waist height. The place smelled musty and unused. Whatever the Superiors were doing here—and Jack was going to get to that—they were not concerned about comfort.

Reaper shoved a door open with his knee and entered a small room, beckoning Jack to follow. Inside were several folding chairs and a table covered with bottles of water, spirits, and tinned food.

"Drink?" Reaper asked. He snatched up a whiskey bottle and spun the top off, tipping it to his mouth and taking several deep glugs. He watched Jack sidelong as he did so, perhaps expecting or hoping for some reaction.

Jack smiled and pushed a memory . . .

The four of them on holiday in Center Parcs. Emily is only a baby in a pushchair, but already she has a laugh that consumes everyone around her. Jack's mother is sitting on a bench feeding Emily an ice cream, and he and his father are paddling a double kayak on the lake. Jack is in front, and with each stroke he deliberately flicks water back at his dad. There is shouting and splashing, and laughter, and as they steer away from the shore Jack feels something pulling him back. He's enjoying this so much, but he wants the four of them to be close together, within touching distance. They all feel like that. It's one of those perfect moments.

Reaper blinked a few times, frowning. Then he slammed the bottle down on the table. "So?"

"Just water," Jack said. Reaper lobbed him a bottle and he caught it one-handed.

"I'm not surprised you came back," Reaper said. "I'm trouble. You seem to be drawn to it like a moth to a flame."

"Fleeter been reporting back to you?"

Reaper nodded.

"Worried about me?"

"No. You interest Miller, and he interests me."

"He's not dead?"

Reaper smiled, and it was horrible. "Oh, I didn't kill him. He won't forget me in a hurry, though."

"So this is a war room," Jack said.

"Just somewhere to hide away," Reaper said. He took another drink of whiskey, and when Jack blinked he lived another memory. But he did not want to push just yet. Reaper was canny, and he might suspect Jack of doing something.

"But the map, the flags. Chopper locations?"

Reaper regarded him for a while, looking him up and down as if he'd never seen him before. It made Jack uncomfortable; a father should know his son so well. "It's a guerrilla war," he said. "Good to keep track of things."

"So if you know where all the Choppers are, why not kill them all?" Jack asked. The idea of it was reprehensible, but he was trying to understand the man his father had become. Or the thing.

"Wendy's talent only goes so far," he said.

"Wendy's the woman working the table out there," Jack said. "She doesn't look like the rest of you. Fleeter. Puppeteer. That shadow guy was out in the tunnels, and I'll bet Scryer isn't that far away."

Reaper gave nothing away.

"Wendy's not a Superior like you, is she? She doesn't think of herself as one anyway."

"She does, actually," Reaper said, leaning back against the table and smiling. "She quickly tired of wandering London, aimless and alone. Sometimes the Irregulars get together in pairs or small groups, but mostly they're just surviving. Not moving on. Evolving."

"Is that what you're doing?" Jack waved one hand at their surroundings.

"We're making plans," Reaper said.

"For what?"

"And why would you need to know that?" Reaper took another drink. This was not the man Jack had expected to find. His father had enjoyed a drink, yes, but Reaper had seemed to be someone different, projecting a disinterest in normal human things. He called himself Superior, yet here he was taking to the bottle.

"Because I need your help," Jack said. "They have Emily and Mum at Camp H."

"Or so Miller told you."

"You think they're somewhere else?"

Reaper barked a loud, mocking laugh. "I don't give a damn where they are, boy! But you can trust Miller as far as you can throw him."

That might be a very long way, Jack thought, because there was a universe inside he had yet to explore. But for now he was enveloped with one power, and he felt it haunting his memory like a name on the tip of his tongue. Soon he would push it to the fore again.

"Here's why I really came back," Jack said. He sat down on one of the folding chairs and stared at his father, trying to see the man he loved. Even his physical features seemed to have changed—hardening, growing grimmer. "The Choppers have Mum and Emily prisoner. They're at Camp H. I have to rescue them, and for that I need your help."

Reaper did not even respond. He snorted a soft laugh and took another drink.

"While we're there, we release everyone else they're holding.

And they've got the girl. The Irregular who works for them, spotting any large groups moving around London."

Reaper hid his surprise well at how much Jack knew. He snorted a laugh again, but Jack saw through the façade, and for a flicker his father was there before him. His eyes opened a little wider, and he scratched at one ear.

"You could stop her," Jack said. "That'd give you London."

"I *have* London," Reaper said. His voice was quiet, but loaded with the awful potential of his murderous power. *One growl and he'll crush me and this chair into a bloody metal mass*, Jack thought.

"Surely that's not all you want," he said.

Reaper looked into the whiskey bottle, acting casual but considering what Jack had said. *Now*, Jack thought, *but just a little*. He took a drink of water to hide his eyes and pushed a memory Reaper's way.

Jack is playing with Emily on Christmas morning. His train set lies half-finished, and he will return to it very soon. But Emily has a new wooden checkers set, and she's been bugging him for a game. So the two of them sit amongst the detritus of Christmas—rolled-up wrapping paper, scattered presents, plastic ties, the remains of popped crackers—and play a game of checkers. Emily is concentrating so hard that her tongue sticks from one corner of her mouth, and Jack has already made one mistake towards helping her win. Delicious smells come from the kitchen. Soft music plays. Jack glances up, and through the half-open kitchen door he sees his parents embracing, leaning against the work surface and spying on him and Emily. He pretends not to have seen them, but their warm, gentle smiles make him smile. Emily takes two of his pieces and whoops in triumph, and Jack knows it is going to be a day to remember.

He lowered the water bottle and wiped his lips. "Whatever it is you want, I want my Mum and Emily back. And we can help each other."

Reaper was silent for a moment, still looking into his bottle. His confident smiled had dropped. For a long moment, not moving or talking, he was Jack's father once more.

"I don't need anyone's help," Reaper said. "A normal child's least of all."

"You know I'm not that," Jack said. "Nomad touched me. Things are changing. I don't know what the future might bring, but I want my family safe."

"And you're putting thoughts in my head," Reaper said.

"Does it matter? It's your reaction to them that's important."

"I have no reaction. I see strangers, that's all. Strangers living normal, boring lives, with their normal, boring children. Pointless lives."

Jack laughed out loud. Reaper, startled, growled softly, and Jack felt a massive unseen hand shove him back into his chair and against the wall. It hurt, but he laughed some more, somehow managing to fill his compressed lungs. *I could fight back*, he thought, circling constellations of power. But he chose not to. Fighting back would give Reaper what he wanted—simplicity. This was far more complex than power and strength.

"You think your family's lives are pointless?" Jack asked, unbelieving. "What have you got? You live like a rat, you're hunted by people who want to chop you to pieces to examine your brains. You think you're special, but you're more normal than anyone! Just a sad man who thinks power is his friend."

Reaper's growl increased, and the pressure shoving Jack against the wall intensified. One shout from the man and Jack would be a smear across the concrete. From living to dead in a blink. How everything he knew and was could be wiped out in an instant terrified him, but it also gave him more determination. His story was far from over, and he would not let the monster his father had become end it.

"And you're my father," he wheezed. "I'm not putting any thoughts into your head now, Dad. But what are you thinking when you see me? When I mention Mum and Emily? What are you thinking?"

Reaper grimaced, baring his teeth and leaning in over Jack as he prepared to unleash his killing shout. On the outside, he was farther away from his father than Jack had ever seen. But inside, something was changing.

Reaper eased back. He was breathing heavily, and he turned back to the bottle-strewn table, snatching up that whiskey bottle and drinking again.

Bloody hell, Jack thought, trying to halt his shaking. It was excitement as well as fear, and so he let it come.

"They're probably dead already," Reaper said.

"I can't just assume that."

"We don't know where Camp H is."

"I'm sure you have an idea," Jack said. But Reaper shook his head.

"I've been trying to find out. But it's protected. Choppers we capture can't tell us. Whatever we do to them, they won't divulge. I've asked them nicely. Beaten them. Burnt them. Sliced them up. But no one's that well trained. Either they've never known where Miller's base is, or they've had something done to them to make them forget."

"And none of your Superiors can find it." He tried not to inject a note of satisfaction into the statement, but it was difficult. Reaper positioned himself as a leader of superhumans, way above and beyond the sad remnants of humanity left in London. But here he was getting steadily drunk and admitting that there were simple acts beyond their means.

"We could if we really wanted to," Reaper said. It sounded like schoolboy bluster, and it was Jack's turn to snort.

"There really aren't many of you, are there? A few of you living underground, planning grand schemes, killing a few soldiers here and there to make yourself feel important. Special."

"Watch your tone, child."

"I'm no child!" Jack whispered, and without even thinking he imbued those words with a hint of the power Reaper himself possessed. They became heavier, harder, seeming to travel farther, and by the time they were uttered they had picked up a deadly momentum. Reaper took a step back and dropped his bottle, and as it smashed at his feet, a dribble of blood ran from his nose.

Jack tried not to show his surprise at what he'd done. Now more than ever was the time to display complete, conscious control. *Because this is the moment everything hinges on*, he thought. *Reaper can choose to fight back, and we'll destroy each other in this room. Or Dad will make himself known.*

But Reaper did neither. He smiled without threat or affection, and dabbed at the blood dribbling from his nose. Unbidden, a slew of memories came to Jack—this man as his father, doing fatherly things and being a solid core around which his life used to proceed. For the past two years that physical core had been absent, but Jack had been able to continue looking after his younger sister precisely because he kept hope alive that he would find his father and mother again. He had found both . . . yet they were both still lost to him.

"I've killed a hundred people for doing far less than that," Reaper said.

"A fine lesson for a father to teach his son," Jack said.

Reaper looked at his blood on his fingers, then up at Jack again. "So I assume you have a plan?"

"Of course," Jack said. "You and the Irregulars, together."

"They've suggested that before. But they're no part of my life or outlook. Weak. Ineffectual."

"And dying," Jack said. "How about you and the Superiors? Any of you sick?"

"We've evolved way beyond human diseases," Reaper said, and Jack could not read him at all.

"They might be weak, but they can help you find Camp H. You and them together. Pooling talents. Feeding off each other's powers, instead of using them to repulse each other. You'll be . . . the New." Jack smiled, pleased at his moment of inspiration. "That's what you'll call yourselves. Work together to find Camp H, rescue Mum and Emily, and get us all out of the city. Then we blow the whistle on everything that's been happening in London. It all changes. Exposure."

Reaper said nothing, but he looked thoughtful.

"If everything stays as it is, everyone will die," Jack said softly. "And death surely isn't the only way out. The New, Dad. It's the only way."

Reaper nodded slowly. "If we do this—and that's 'if'—we'll need to congregate without being seen."

"Yes," Jack said. "I've thought about that. And I've got it covered."

"You have?" Reaper said. *Well done, Son,* Jack wanted him to continue. *I'm proud of you, Jack. You're grown into a strong young man, even though I wasn't there to . . .*

Jack glanced away, feeling tears threatening. When he looked back, Reaper was watching him, smiling.

"What?" Jack asked harshly.

"You're interesting. Impressive. Maybe you'll be as much a Superior as me."

"No," Jack said. "I might be able to do things, but you know what? I'm just a normal boy."

He would have liked to believe that. As they left the room and

Reaper spoke to a couple of his people, Jack did his best to find the truth in the statement. But when he knocked and entered the small room where Sparky and Jenna were resting, and saw them both glance up at him with momentary fear in their eyes, he knew that they had been talking about him, and that he was moving farther away from normal with every breath he drew.

CHAPTER NINE
THE WILD

Nomad never slept, but still she dreamed. These moments came at calmer times when she remained motionless for a while, letting her limbs and body settle and her mind wander. She would drift, and return, and she had always assumed that what she saw were echoes from her earlier life. Memories shaded by the change within her. She had been something far different before Evolve.

But recently she had been dreaming of the girl with purple hair . . .

She walks towards Nomad along a lush riverbank of waving reeds and gorgeous orchids. Hummingbirds flit from bloom to bloom, bees buzz in the sunlight, and the grass underfoot is soft and healthy. There are straight edges and corners somewhere, but mostly out of sight. The verdant growth is the future, and it is a fitting cloak with which to mask the less-perfect present. Nomad goes along with it, even though she knows it is a lie. Even though she knows that the present is her fault.

The girl reaches for her and calls. But then Nomad sees something—her stance, her face, the way her fingers claw at the air—that promises only pain. The girl is desperate, yet Nomad turns away.

Light dawns. The explosion blasts away the plants, flowers, and hummingbirds, and as they are scorched to nothing they revert to their true forms—melting metal, flying glass, flaming things scarring the air.

The purple-haired girl screams at her. Nomad moves towards the blast, hoping that she can stop it. But no one is that special.

The girl promised fire and death. Nomad had no sense that her random dreams were visions of the future, and yet they could surely be nothing else? She had never seen the girl before, and now knew that she existed. What was that if not prophecy?

The explosion would kill everyone. That, Nomad did not mind. She had killed so many through her actions, and more would only add to her damned tally.

But . . .

I cannot allow Jack to die. He is my greatest hope, the pure version of every impurity I seeded. He has to survive to make everything right. And perhaps . . . perhaps for Jack to survive, the girl has to die.

The cries of inhuman things welcomed them to the north. They were awful, alien sounds, and they set Lucy-Anne's nerves on edge. First from one direction, then another, they seemed to sing across the dark city, imparting secrets that everyone but she knew, and however much she tried to deny it, she could not shake the idea that she was at their centre. The shrieks had an intelligence to them that she found disconcerting, and Rook had no answer when she whispered her fears. That he was also troubled made everything that much worse.

She had rarely ever experienced true night. Society steered away from darkness, consciously or not. During the day the sun stood watch overhead, but at night there was need for artificial suns to keep at bay those demons and monsters from less enlightened times. In the village where she'd lived alone for two years since Doomsday there were street lamps, exterior lights on houses, and the cool borrowed glare of TVs behind curtains, all of which bathed village streets and gave them at least a pretence at daylight. Since the tragedy that consumed London, the worst monsters had been on the inside. Perhaps they always had been. So fending off darkness with artificial light was a token gesture that was easy to make.

Here in the wilder, most deadly north of London, darkness had found a home. With a newly overcast sky there was barely any light at all, and their surroundings existed beneath a diffused night-sky sheen. Shadows watched them from everywhere.

Lucy-Anne held Rook's hand tightly as they walked through the tree-lined streets of Primrose Hill. She feared that if she let go she might lose him; he and his rooks wore the night rather than drawing back from it. She could see him only because he was close, and she could not see the birds at all. They were shadows wafting by her cheeks, or occasionally cawing from above.

The avenue's trees were little more than ghostly stumps, the street's uneven surfaces broken with creeping weeds, vehicles wrecked like the memories of long ago. It seemed that the farther north they came, the farther back in memory a healthy London existed.

Maybe they can change time, Lucy-Anne thought. *Maybe everything is older here now. They're gone ahead, evolved even more, and we're invading somewhere we should never be.*

"We're being watched," Rook said softly, and without slowing down.

"By what?"

"I don't know. Just keep moving."

Lucy-Anne looked around but could see only shadows within shadows. But though sight was stolen by the almost-unnatural dark, she could still smell the stench of beasts.

The terrible, shattering idea that Andrew could be one of these had already hit home, though she refused the idea time to take root. It was simply out of the question that her brother had survived only to become a monster. If that had happened, everything about him would have changed. Those people they had seen in the park were barely human, and the sense of things around them now was truly alien, and other.

The man in the hotel had sensed Andrew as part of her bloodline. And the strange woman Sara had narrowed his smell to Hampstead Heath. Surely they would not have been able to do that if he had not remained human?

But in truth, she did not know. She was clutching at straws.

"How far to Hampstead Heath?" she asked.

"Couple of miles." Rook's reply was clipped, stressed. She squeezed his hand but received nothing in response.

A rook landed on her shoulder. Its claws dug in and she winced, but did not cry out. She turned, face-to-face with the bird, and in the faint light she could just see its head jerking left and right. Another landed beside it, and the two of them flapped their wings to try and maintain purchase on her jacket, wings whispering across her face. More landed on Rook—two on each shoulder, one on his head, and then two more when he extended his free arm.

"What?" Lucy-Anne whispered.

"Scared," Rook said, and she wasn't sure whether he meant himself or his birds.

More birds drifted down low, fluttering as they attempted to fly as close to Rook as possible, and soon her vision was obscured by shadows that moved rather than those that hid. Her dream came back to her—the birds attacking her—but she knew this was far from that. This was something worse.

Rook started running, pulling Lucy-Anne with him. His grip hurt her but it was a welcome pain. Secure. She could not imagine letting go and losing him in this darkness, where anything might dwell.

Shrieks came again, closer this time. And for the first time she thought perhaps they came from above.

"Flying things," she said, and Rook's brief squeeze confirmed that he already knew.

Something passed above them. Lucy-Anne gasped and looked up, unsure how she had sensed it—smell, or motion, or sight, or perhaps a combination. She saw nothing, but the sense of being watched increased to an overwhelming extent, and she waved her free arm over her head, terrified that she would feel something above her. There was only air.

The rooks started *caw-caw*ing, flapping their wings but not taking off. Lucy-Anne squinted as a wings slapped across her eyes and stung, blinding her for a moment. It made little difference. She blinked rapidly until she could see again, and Rook was steering them across the street towards a hulking shape.

More shapes passed overhead, and something reached down and snatched at Lucy-Anne's hair. She screamed as a tuft of hair was ripped from her head, and felt the warmth of fresh blood spreading across her scalp.

Rook whistled, and above them Lucy-Anne heard rooks impacting something larger and more vicious. Birds cried out and immediately started raining down around them, broken and torn. She stepped on one and felt the gentle give as its bones crumbled beneath her foot.

"I'm sorry, I'm sorry," she said. Rook tugged hard on her hand, urging her onward.

More birds swooped in and something else screeched above and to the left. It was a terrible sound—pained, angry, and undeniably human.

"In here!" Rook said. He shoved her towards the shadow, and she saw it was a vehicle of some kind. The door scraped as he pulled it open, then she was thrust unceremoniously into the driver's seat and the door slammed behind her.

Silence. And the smell of decay.

"Oh my God," Lucy-Anne whispered. The passenger door was opened, the sudden sound making her jump, and Rook tumbled in. He held the door for a moment and whistled again, and the inside of the car was suddenly filled with flapping, panicked shapes. He closed the door, the shapes quickly settled, and the silence was shocking.

Something scraped along the roof, like nails on a blackboard. Lucy-Anne shrunk down in the seat, holding her head, bending forward, wishing that everything would go away. *I'm back in Camp Truth with Jack,* she thought. *We've just woken up from a snooze, I've dreamed all of this,* all *of it, and there's an hour before Sparky and Jenna will arrive. We'll kiss each other, and perhaps more. We can do whatever we want, because I'm just so glad this was all a dream!*

But it was not a dream. The big flying things were circling the car and skittering their claws across the roof. And inside the car, something dead sat behind her.

Rook spoke as soon as she shifted.

"Don't look back," he said.

"Can they get in?"

"I don't know." He sounded calm, but he was looking around like a startled bird.

The urge to turn around was huge. She could smell the mustiness of old decay, a stench that had become familiar since she'd entered London with her friends, and she knew that someone dead shared the car with them. *Or we're sharing their car,* she thought. *Sorry. Sorry to sit in your car.*

Then she saw the key in the ignition, and her thoughts of the dead person vanished.

"I can drive this," she said.

"What? No! Don't be ridiculous."

"Hey, there's plenty you don't know about me. I've nicked a car or two. Can drive. Even if the key wasn't there, I could probably start the thing given time."

"No," Rook said, and he grabbed her shoulder. It was a surprising gesture, but one she welcomed. "I mean, no one drives cars apart from the Choppers. Too dangerous. Too easy to see or hear."

"You really think there are Choppers here to see or hear?" she asked.

He was watching her in the darkness. She could just make out the faint glint of his eyes, and his shadows sitting beside her was solid reality. Everything else was ambiguous.

Claws raked across the car roof again, and something big flitted in front of the windscreen.

"Whatever, I'm not going out there," Lucy-Anne said. A dozen of his birds had entered the car with them, and glancing in the rearview mirror she could see several silhouetted against the rear window. She also caught sight of a larger shape and glanced away again.

"Try," Rook said at last. "The battery will be flat. The tyres will be down. Water in the engine. Something."

Lucy-Anne grabbed the key and felt the fob, running her fingers over the cold metal. "Mazda," she said. "Mum and Dad always swore by them." She made sure the car was out of gear and turned the key. The engine coughed, hacked a few times, and then caught. She pressed on the gas and revved. The car vibrated with restrained power.

"Wow," Rook said.

"Yeah," Lucy-Anne said. "Well. Where to, sir?" Laughing softly, she turned on the headlights. The street before them was flooded with weak light and she gasped with shock.

Three shapes squatted on the broken road, flinching away from the light. They were humanoid, but their bodies were thin and stringy, bare skin pale and diseased, and open sores wept across their abdomens and legs. They had what looked like stumpy wings, useless and malformed. Their faces were bulbous, each feature exaggerated. They looked like gargoyles.

"Oh my . . ." Lucy-Anne muttered. The gargoyle-people fled, scampering from the haze of weak headlamps and finding shadows once more

"Unnatural," Rook said. He seemed deeply troubled, his face creased in an intense frown in the pale dashboard light. "Not right. That's not right."

"Can't argue with you there," Lucy-Anne said, and she slipped the car into first gear. It moved sluggishly, heavily, and she admitted to herself that Rook had been right on one count; at least one tyre was flat. But she moved eventually into third gear and drove slowly along the road, and the gargoyle-people did not trouble them again. Perhaps they had climbed and now hung overhead, watching. Maybe they squatted on rooftops and watched the car moving northward, pushing a pool of weak light before it. Lucy-Anne's world became the splash of light ahead of them, and the inside of the car, and the place somewhere beyond both where her brother was still alive.

Not like that, she thought. *Not with wings and a face like that! Not with withered arms so he can snake along the ground. Not with scales or fur, not changed at all, but just . . . Andrew.* She wished she could fall asleep and dream him well. But since the vision of the nuclear explosion and Nomad's casual presence, she had been afraid to sleep at all.

"I need something to eat," she said. "A drink. Water. Something."

"Soon," Rook said.

"How do you know?"

"I don't. Never been this far north. But we'll get something soon."

"What, bird seed?" Her voice grew louder and tinged with panic, so she gripped the wheel harder and concentrated, breathing long and deep. Losing it again would do no one any good. "What happened to them?" she asked at last.

"Don't know. Extreme reaction to Doomsday."

"Extreme?" Loud again, panicked. She slammed the wheel with one hand and they veered to the left, clipping the side of a parked van.

"I've only heard the rumours," he said. "Never wanted to see for myself."

"Why?"

"Didn't want to see what I might have become."

They fell silent. Lucy-Anne concentrated on her driving, pleased when the glare of headlights grew stronger as the battery was charged again. It was amazing that the car had started so quickly after two years, and she wanted to tell someone about that—Jack, Sparky, Jenna. But that opportunity might not come again.

She weaved the car along the streets, passing between parked or crashed vehicles when she could, working to shove a path through when she could not. She quickly learned that low gear and low revs was best for pushing an obstacle out of the way, but several times they had to backtrack to find an alternative route. Sometimes this took them into narrow side streets or even the back lanes between house gardens, and perhaps it was a trick of the light, but she saw many shadows darting away.

We're being watched all the time, she thought. It was a chilling idea. But it didn't matter. Andrew was somewhere ahead of her, always ahead. Soon, she hoped, she would find him. And then this part of her journey would be over.

What came next would depend on who or what Andrew had become.

"I never thought I'd see you scared," Lucy-Anne said. Dawn was breaking across the rooftops to the east, and Hampstead Heath was close. Their journey had been slow but uninterrupted, a mummified corpse sat in the seat behind her, and a dozen rooks perched around the car, swaying in time with its movement and occasionally calling out for no apparent reason. It was a surreal journey, and she needed it broken.

"What, you think I'm some sort of super human?"

"Don't you?"

Rook smiled. It was the first time she'd seen him smiling since dusk the previous evening, and it looked good on him.

"I feel . . ." He sighed, and a rook hopped down from his shoulder onto his knee. It pecked at a fly buzzing the window, its beak striking the glass with a musical *tink*!

"Feel what?"

"Different. I feel different."

"You *are* different."

"And abandoned. Do you have any idea what it's like? Can you even think about how it felt after Doomsday, when London was filled with dead people and I was left . . . alone. We survived for a time, me and my brother. We thought there'd be rescue attempts. But then they took him, and I was alone, and I knew that was it. So yeah, I'm different. I've moved on. London's the whole world now, but that doesn't mean I don't sometimes get scared. Doesn't everyone?"

"Everyone human, yeah. Dunno about the Superiors." She glanced sidelong at him when she said this, but she already knew what he thought about them. He was as much Superior as he was Irregular. Rook was one of the few who was completely his own person. His only allegiance was to his birds.

And now perhaps to her as well.

"Slow down," he said. "Need to find out where we are."

She slowed the car at a road junction but left it running, and Rook opened his window. The rooks in the car with them took flight immediately, flitting through the window and spiralling up above the car. Lucy-Anne leaned over the steering wheel and looked up, but they were quickly lost to dawn's glare.

"So what else have you heard about the north?" she asked. "Those weird gargoyle people. And snake people. I've seen nothing like them before."

"Just that it's where the monsters came." A bird fluttered through the window and landed on his shoulder, and moments later he glanced at Lucy-Anne. "Hampstead Heath's half a mile from here."

"Half a mile." If that Sara woman was right . . . if Andrew was still alive, and not changed like those other weird things . . . if Rook was telling her the truth.

"Maybe we should walk from here," he said.

"Yeah," Lucy-Anne said. A distance was growing around her. She frowned and ground a knuckle into her thigh to wake herself up.

"Or perhaps a rest." Rook's voice was farther away now.

"No time," she said. "No time to . . ." But her eyelids drooped, and she could not remember the last time she'd had a good sleep. The release of stress now that she'd stopped driving the car allowed her weariness to the fore.

"Don't worry," she heard him say, and his hand was warm on her arm. "I'll look after you." His voice, so distant; his words, such a comfort.

She was already dreaming as she fell asleep, and the woman was waiting for her.

She feels Andrew close by but can't find him. His presence is overwhelming, as though he has just spoken to her or given her a playful pinch on the arm, like he used to when they were kids. She turns a full circle and expects to see him at any moment, but nothing around her is normal.

A dream.

At first she is alone. The sense of Andrew is strong, but it's as if he has been found and lost again, and suddenly he is a memory once more. She sobs out loud. So unfair.

She is somewhere wild in this old city. The undergrowth is overgrown and lush, luxuriating in freedom from shears and mowers—grass touches her shins, shrubs hang heavy, tree limbs have fallen across barely visible paths. Once this might have been a pleasant place to wander and reflect, but now it is back with nature.

I'm dreaming . . .

She walks towards a vague structure in the distance. It is artificial, she is sure, but its edges are blurred with ivy and time. Shapes around it might once have been picnic tables, but they've fallen into disrepair and been subsumed beneath rampant plant growth. There is a flash of colour inside, a hint of movement. She is troubled but excited, and deep inside she knows who and what this is.

But the Lucy-Anne in her dream—bearing her consciousness, carrying her mind—is a different person. She walks towards the building, even though she knows she should flee. She raises a hand and waves, attracting the attention of the woman inside, even though she is dreadfully aware of what will come next.

No . . . turn . . . run . . .

The strange woman parts a curtain of beautiful hanging plants and emerges from the building. She's dressed plainly, yet even set against the gorgeous flowers she is stunning. Her hair drifts around her head like she is forever falling, her face is serene, and as she turns away a small smile lights her features. But the smile is not for Lucy-Anne, because the woman starts walking away.

She skirts around the building and moves quickly into the park.

Wait! Lucy-Anne tries to shout, but she has no voice.

Call her . . . make a voice . . . this is my dream and I must—

The flash. Unbearably bright, it shadows the woman from every direction and scorches her silhouette into the ground all around her. Leaves wither, flowers crumple, branches snap, and trees fall. A firestorm rips through the park and scorches everything to charcoal, and then the blast takes it apart. But the woman still stands, untouched and untouchable.

And Lucy-Anne feels the terrible truth of this scene.

In the distance a mushroom cloud deforms the sky, and there is a breath-stealing sense of time running out.

"I'm dreaming!" she shouted, and Rook was holding her arms, leaning in the driver's door and shaking her awake. Her eyes snapped open and she looked up at him, so pleased that he was there. She breathed easier. "I'm dreaming."

"No more," he said, and he seemed excited. "Come on. You gotta see this." Then he was away, and she had to leap from the car and start running to keep up with him.

Daylight seemed kinder to this part of London. Shaking the horrors of her dream, she hoped that the day would be kind to her.

CHAPTER TEN
JOINING FORCES

"**B**ack to Breezer?" Sparky spat. "Are you out of your tiny, birdlike bloody mind?"

"Probably," Jack said, nodding. "Maybe." He was looking at Jenna, expecting a reaction from her as well. But she was grim-faced and silent. She seemed to understand, and he was impressed once again with his friend's quiet intelligence.

"Why? We almost killed ourselves escaping him and coming here, now you want to go *back*?"

"Reaper doesn't know where Camp H is."

"Like hell!" Sparky said.

"Really?" Jenna frowned, then nodded slowly. "If he did, he'd have hit it long before now."

"I'm guessing so," Jack said. He sighed and sat down, taking a long swig from a mug of tea. There was food on the small table in their room as well—tinned beans, potatoes—but he didn't feel hungry.

"So . . ." Sparky said, tapping a finger against his chin as he thought, "you persuaded your dad to join forces with Irregulars."

"I don't think I persuaded him to do anything. I made the suggestion and gave my reasons, and he saw some use in the idea. I think he saw me, and Mum and Emily, as a way to save face. If he went to the Irregulars on his own, it'd be like admitting he needs their help. Doing it this way, he can say it's me who needs the help."

"Well, it is," Jenna said.

"Yeah," Sparky said. "Loser."

Jack went for him. A dig in the thigh gave Sparky a dead leg, but as Jack tried to get him in a headlock, Sparky twisted and reversed the position. His arm closed around Jack's throat, and he rubbed the top of his head with his knuckles. It hurt, but Jack felt wonderful. For a moment it was as if nothing had changed.

"Use your deadly powers against me if you will, but I will always triumph!" Sparky said. He ran his knuckles across Jack's scalp again.

"Ow!" Jack said, his voice muffled. "You bastard, that—"

"Resistance is futile!"

"Yeah, right," Jack said, and he relaxed, then drove his fist into Sparky's thigh again. They tumbled to the floor together, wrestling, laughing, and catching sight of Jenna rolling her eyes only made Jack laugh some more.

"Kids," she said. As Jack and Sparky's laughter died down and they sat up, Jenna looked at Jack softly and asked, "So. Your dad?"

Jack breathed heavily, catching his breath. He felt tears threaten, and a surprising rush of emotions flooded through him. His friends watched expectantly, and they were the good friends they'd always been, no matter what was happening to him. He knew that they feared him. But he was also starting to fear himself.

"He's still there," Jack said. "I did something to him. Forced some memories onto him, good times we had as a family. I sort of . . . pressed them in while we were talking."

"And?" Jenna asked.

"And for a moment, he looked like my dad again." Jack didn't feel as pleased as he should have.

"But you want him to be your dad without you doing anything," Sparky said.

"Yeah," Jack said, nodding. Sparky had it in one. "Yeah, course I do."

"Well, we're mixed up with him again now," Jenna said. "Maybe when he sees your mum."

"Or Emily," Sparky said. "How could he fail to love Emily?"

"It's all so shit," Jack said softly. "Who'd have thought it would have come to this?"

"We knew what we were doing when we came in," Jenna said.

"No," Sparky said. "We didn't. Not a clue. We came because we were desperate."

The three of them fell silent at that, because Sparky was right. Jack had been desperate to discover the fate of his parents, Sparky his brother, and Jenna had come because of what the Choppers had done to her father—arrested because of his investigations into Doomsday, and returned a changed, lesser man.

That's why we came, Jack thought. *We had no intention of leading a crusade.*

"So you're going to ask Breezer and his people to help your dad," Jenna said.

"Between Breezer and Reaper and their people, they should be able to discover the location of Camp H," Jack said.

"So how do we do that and avoid detection by the Choppers?" Sparky asked.

Jack smiled. This was where it got interesting.

Dawn across a silent London, and a glorious sunrise gave the cityscape the look of an expressionist painting. Clouds boiled pink, looking beautiful and promising rain, and the city was sheened with promise. *If I didn't know any better I might take it as a sign*, Jack thought. But in these strange times, perhaps that was exactly what it was.

"Gorgeous," Sparky said.

"Girl," Jenna said. He nudged her in the ribs, she pinched his arm. Then they leaned in together, keeping contact and taking comfort. Jack experienced a fleeting memory of him and Lucy-Anne when they had still been close. He didn't think whatever had been between them had been anything like this.

"What?" Jenna asked self-consciously.

"You two," Jack said. His friends glanced at each other.

"I took pity on her," Sparky said. "Someone had to love her."

"He's such a loser, he needs looking after," Jenna said.

You going to stand here farting around all day? The voice came from behind Jack, and when he glanced back he saw a shadow moving away from him, flowing against the old market's front façade. Shade. Even his voice was like a shadow, a thing not truly there. When Reaper had called Shade to him and told him what was happening, Jack had shaken his hand, and it had felt . . . not quite there. He was nothing like Fleeter. She was solid and real, and able to shift between blinks and heartbeats. Shade was something that Evolve had moved to a different realm of reality. He was out of synch, and when Jack had squeezed his hand he'd felt a moment of sickening vertigo, as if he was about to tumble an unimaginable distance. *Perhaps I could find his talent within me*, he'd thought, *but I really don't want to.*

"No," Jack said. "We're going."

"Don't like him as a bodyguard," Sparky said. "Spooky bastard." He didn't bother keeping his voice down.

"We're taking Breezer what he wants, surely?" Jenna said. "Hooking up with the Superiors?"

"Maybe," Jack said. "But I think since meeting me, he might want me more."

They set off. Shade moved with them, and sometimes he was as visible as someone normal. He wore jeans, a shirt, and a jacket, all black, and his short cropped hair was the same colour. His skin was very pale. He did not smile. The world seemed to weigh on his shoulders, and Jack wondered whether gravity had become his enemy.

More often, Jack caught sight of Shade from the corner of his eye. Then he would be a shadow brought to life, flowing through the streets like darkness given form. Sparky and Jenna were jumpy, and Jack knew they were seeing the same thing.

They were probably wondering whether Jack could do that, too.

It felt strange approaching the skyscraper they had so recently escaped. Yesterday they had leaped from the roof of this building in a rickety hang glider, trusting their lives to fate. Coming back made the memory of that escape unreal.

"Bloody high, isn't it?" Sparky said.

"We'd have made a mess on the pavement." Jenna was clasping Sparky's hand, and Jack could not shake the growing feeling that he was alone. Left out. He hated it, because there was a selfishness to that thought.

"It might be best if you . . ." Jack started saying, but Shade was no longer there. They heard breaking glass from somewhere, a shout, and then several more voices joining in. They sounded confused and scared.

"So much for diplomacy," Sparky said.

"Come on," Jack said. "I'm hoping this'll be pretty easy."

The three men and two women on the ground floor of the office building let them pass when they saw Jack. They were all surprised, but he also saw an element of respect as well. Maybe their daring escape had livened up these people's day.

They climbed, and Shade led the way. He flowed up the stairs, moving from shadow to shadow and making it appear that the stairwell was flexing and bulging, some monstrous gullet sucking them upwards. After fifteen storeys doors started opening behind them as they passed, and faces peered into the stairwell to watch them go. Several people followed them, including two women bearing rifles. But no one spoke.

Breezer was waiting for them on the twentieth floor. He leaned against the stair railing, looking down casually as they climbed the last flight towards him. They were panting hard, sweating from the climb, and Jack had been ignoring the temptation to dip into his powers to find something to help. His friends could not do that. He wanted to work as hard as them.

They stopped on the landing. Shade was a flight below them, standing in the corner and almost not there. He said nothing, only watched. The threat exuding from him was overt and did not require voicing.

"You owe me a hang glider," Breezer said.

"Bill me," Sparky said. "My address is 55 Don't-give-a-shit Avenue."

Breezer looked past them at Shade and quickly looked away again.

"You told me you weren't really the leader here," Jack said. "I'm hoping that was a lie."

"Hoping?"

Jack sighed, probed, grasped a point of light inside, squeezed it tight. A rush of information. He used Breezer's talent against him. "It's how the others see you," he said. "You're strong. Resourceful. And you never were a heating engineer."

"Oh," Breezer said. "Well. That's a pretence I've kept up since Doomsday."

"So what was he?" Jenna asked.

"Police," Jack said. "Serious Organised Crime squad."

"Amazing," Breezer said. "How do you do it? What does it feel like?"

"Unnatural," Jack said. He closed his mind to what Nomad had given him and spat, trying to rid himself of her taste.

"Hungry?" Breezer asked.

"Burgers?" Sparky asked hopefully.

Breezer laughed. It was such a natural, unforced sound that it put Jack instantly at ease, and he glanced back at Shade and gestured.

"Come on," Jack said. "You do eat, don't you?"

Not so anyone would notice.

"Fine." Jack followed Sparky and Jenna through the doorway, and as it swung shut he saw Shade slip through from the corner of his eye. Their guard. Jack was already quite certain he would not be required.

The same cooking barrel, the same people around them, but this time Breezer seemed more deferential. He had underestimated Jack and his friends last time. Now, they had proved themselves more resourceful than he could have imagined.

"So you went to your father," Breezer said. He glanced around the open-plan office, looking for Shade. Dawn sunlight bathed them, casting shadows behind screens and in doorways, and Shade could have been anywhere. "Got one of his monsters protecting you."

"They're not monsters," Jack said.

"Then what are they?" Breezer asked.

"Confused," Jenna said. "They're overwhelmed. Everything changed so quickly. They lost loved ones, saw what became of millions in London, lived amongst the stink and rot of decaying bodies. Then they were hunted and murdered, and they fought back. One of them can . . . I don't know how, but she slows time. Jumps between moments. They're at odds with their humanity. They're not monsters. They've just had these powers thrust upon them, and they don't know how to handle them."

"Haven't we all?" Breezer asked.

"Yes," Jenna said, glancing at Jack. "And I think you all might be fighting madness."

"Charming," Breezer said, but he did not dispute what she'd said.

"I told you what my priority was," Jack said. "My mother, my sister. *Everyone* they've got at Camp H. Well, now there might be a way to get to them."

"You've asked Reaper for help," Breezer said. "And he said yes?"

"He's agreed that by combining talents, you might be able to find Camp H."

"And can't you do it?" Breezer asked. "Nomad's touch is on you, Jack. Isn't it? Can't you just sit there now and find Camp H?"

"No," Jack said. "It's not that easy."

"Why not?"

"Because I'm still learning." And he was convinced that was the truth. He had used a power similar to Breezer's because the man had been close, and his star had shone brighter in Jack's mind's eye. But he could not do everything. Not yet.

He saw something in Breezer's eyes then that he had already glimpsed in his friends': fear. He didn't like it at all.

"And how do we . . ." Breezer waved a hand about, indicating the Irregulars who shared the building with him. "How do we all meet with Reaper and his 'Superiors,' and not get spied by the bitch working for the Choppers."

Jack looked around at them all. Sparky was tucking into a burger, big and burly and making loud chomping sounds, but Jack saw him glancing left and right, alert for the first sign of danger. Jenna sat close to Sparky, and though she was frowning, she gave Jack a brief smile that said, *I trust you.*

"That's something for me and Reaper to know," Jack said. "I'll give you a location and a time. That's all."

Breezer laughed, saw that Jack was serious, and stood slowly from the office chair.

"You expect me to accept that?" he asked.

"Yes," Jack said. "It's the element of surprise that will make this work, and the more people who know, the more likely we lose the surprise."

Breezer shook his head and turned away, walking towards the glazed wall so that dawn threw his shadow back at them. He conversed with two of his people, and after a few moments his shoulders relaxed, and Jack knew that he had relented. Breezer's companions looked at Jack with something akin to wonder.

Don't be amazed by me, he thought. *Don't fear me*. Not for the first time, he wished he could shrug off Nomad's touch and rid himself of the memory of her taste. But doing so would be like changing his whole self. And no one really changed.

That was something he was banking on.

No one really changed.

Reaper had chosen the most innocuous, unlikely of places, and Jack had taken him on trust. He had no choice. If Reaper and his Superiors meant harm to Jack and his friends, they could have murdered them ten times over. If they had cruel plans for Breezer and the few Irregulars allied to him, they could doubtless have tracked them down, tortured them, killed them. Jack could only assume that Reaper's aim now matched his own—the discovery of Camp H.

The name Hope would take on a whole new meaning today.

"Well, this is nice," Sparky said. "All we need now is an ice cream with one of those crumbly chocolate fingers stuck in it. And sprinkles, of course. Gotta have them."

"Yeah," Jenna said. "Must have sprinkles. What's the point of ice cream if you don't?"

"Precisely!" Sparky said. "Just what I've always said. Jack?"

"Flakey chocolate, yes. But on the sprinkles issue, I'm in neither camp," Jack said. "I can take them or leave them, to be honest."

Jenna and Sparky looked at him as if he was mad. Sparky's mouth hung open.

"You're weird," Jenna said.

"Tell me about it," Jack said.

They had righted a broken table and some chairs and were sitting on a wide pavement area outside a café in Covent Garden. Sparky had found three cans of flat lemonade and they were taking small sips, listening out for anyone approaching. Shade was somewhere nearby. Jack had seen him following them from Breezer's office block, glimpsing him from the corner of his eye. But there was no telling where he was now. He could have been inside one of the surrounding buildings—clothes stores, cafés, music shops, shoe shops, places of fashion and grace that meant little now—or perhaps he was closer by. Because even in the glare of day, this was a city of shadows. The cars had been motionless for so long, the shops undisturbed, that shadows seemed to have taken on some strange solidity.

They sat silently for a while, sipping their drinks, and it might have been the first time they'd been this still out in the open since entering London. Jack leaned back in his chair and thought about that—they'd always been running or hiding or seeing terrible things. Now, he could hear how silent this once-vibrant city had become.

A breeze rustled litter along the street. A door creaked open and closed. A bird of prey called somewhere in the distance. But the silence was louder.

"This just sucks," Sparky said. Jack nodded without looking at his friend. Sparky had survived these past two years by believing that his brother might still be alive. He'd discovered that was not the case, and Jack was amazed at how well he had taken the news. Jenna had helped with that, Jack knew, and he was delighted that the two of them had come together at last. But it also showed that his burly, loud friend was perhaps more sensitive than them all.

"Yeah," Jack said. "But it won't always be like this."

"Can you be so sure?" Jenna asked.

"Yeah, is that like . . . seeing the future?"

"I can't do that," Jack said. "Don't think *anyone* can do that."

"Can't say that," Sparky said. "Don't know what else in London we haven't seen yet."

"You okay?" Jack asked. Sparky looked up at him, staring into his eyes as he drained his can and belched.

"Never better."

"We'll all get home," Jack said. "I promise, Sparky. All of us."

"Well . . ." Sparky said, shrugging, holding Jenna's hand across the table, showing that he was nowhere near "never better."

"Home can never be the same again," Jenna said.

Jack went to disagree, but he knew that she was right. There was a simple truth in her words. As ever, Jenna was wise.

"Every step of the way, things have been changing," Jenna said. "*We've* been changing. If we do all get back home, what then? Sparky's brother's dead. Lucy-Anne is missing. And you're . . ." She nodded at Jack, then looked away.

"Changing," Sparky said. "You're changing so much, mate. What'll you do back at home?"

Jack blinked and tried to imagine being there with Emily— getting her off to school, doing the washing, working his two small jobs to try to bring in enough money to feed them both. And he could not picture it. It all seemed so mundane now that he could make himself and his friends unseen, heat metal up with the power of his mind, glean the truth from lies, and all those other talents he had yet to discover. He blinked slowly and witnessed the universe of possibilities Nomad had given him, and that was real life now. The star-rich place where every point of light was something amazing . . . *that* was home.

"You'll always be my best mates," he said, admitting that everything was different.

"Yeah," Jenna said.

"Pussy," Sparky said.

Jack smiled.

"Company," Sparky said softly.

"Where?" Jack asked.

"Someone watching from that café window. What, you didn't detect them with your Spidey senses?"

"Eat me. Who is it?"

"You won't taste as good as those burgers. Someone dressed in black. Looks like your old man."

Jack stood and turned around to look at the café, making it very clear that they knew the watcher was there. This wasn't Shade, of that he was sure. It was someone surveying the ground before emerging.

Jack waved. The figure didn't move, and for a moment he thought perhaps it was a trick of the light. Then the shadow shifted, and seconds later the café door screeched open.

Reaper emerged. He looked around the street and grinned. *He's so bloody confident*, Jack thought, and that was another aspect alien to his father. His dad had been a humble man, never confident in much of what he did. *He could never please his own father*, Jack's mother had told him once when he'd asked about this, and it was an answer he had never wanted elaborated. Jack had always done his best to please his parents, and they had always been full of praise for him.

"Hi, Dad," Jack said. Reaper raised an eyebrow but did not reply.

"Dude, that black coat thing . . ." Sparky said. He trailed off, chuckling, and Jack threw him a sharp glance.

"Glad I amuse you," Reaper said.

"Yeah, well."

Reaper growled. It was almost sub-audible, like rocks grinding together in the depths of the earth, and the table they had been sitting at flipped onto its side. Jenna fell backwards in her chair, and Sparky stood and stumbled back.

"We don't need this!" Jack said. The strength in his own voice surprised him, and deep down he touched the star that might give him his father's power. But it was a sickening touch, repulsive. A power simply for destruction. He wasn't sure he could ever bring himself to fully use something like that.

Reaper sighed and looked around as if nothing had happened.

Jenna stood and Sparky went to her, but she pushed him away. Jack watched until they both caught his gaze, then he pursed his lips and shook his head.

"Your friend not here yet?" Reaper asked.

"Twenty minutes," Jack said, glancing at his watch. "I thought we'd agreed—"

"I arrive and depart to my own schedule," Reaper said. He seemed to be avoiding looking at Jack. Maybe that was a good sign—that he felt uncomfortable looking at the son he was doing his best to shun—or perhaps it was simply that he could never care again.

Jack could have pushed another memory onto him. There were a thousand good times he had grasped hold of since Doomsday, but now they all felt very personal to him. The more memories he pushed onto Reaper, the more sullied they became.

Besides, that was cheating. His father still possessed his own mind, and it would surely be best and more honest if he decided for himself.

They spent a strange twenty minutes waiting for Breezer and his people to arrive. Sparky and Jenna stood close together, whispering, immersed in their own private world. Jack righted the table and sat down again, trying to act calm and slow his galloping heart. Reaper strolled. He never passed out of sight, but neither did he stop close to them for long.

Jack watched, and several times he almost stood and went to talk to him. But there was little left to say. Reaper had come, and from that Jack took as much comfort as he could. Surely, at least a small part of what Reaper was doing was in an effort to rescue his wife and daughter? Jack could only hope.

Breezer appeared right on time. Four people came with him, and though Jack had seen them all in the office block, he did not know their names. Two men and two women, none of them hiding their nervousness. They only had eyes for Reaper.

"Thank you," Jack said, standing to welcome Breezer. He extended his hand, and Breezer looked surprised. He took Jack's hand and shook.

"I wasn't expecting to see him," he said, inclining his head towards where Reaper was standing in front of an old clothing shop. The window was shattered, naked mannequins splayed across the floor and pavement like moss-covered corpses.

"It bugs him that he's never been able to find Camp H," Jack said.

"It would. He's Superior." Breezer seemed nervous, but also retained some of the qualities that seemed to have made him de facto leader of this small group of Irregulars. He exuded strength and confidence, and Jack knew he would be calm under pressure. "So now what?"

"Nine of us here together, at least," Jack said. "You think . . . ?"

"I'm pretty sure she'll see nine, especially out in the open," Breezer said.

"Hope so."

"Your plan depends on that?"

"Yeah."

Breezer nodded, smiled. "Sounds pretty uncertain to me."

"Yeah," Jack said again, and he smiled back. "That's me all over."

Breezer's smile seemed heartfelt and honest, and Jack began to hope he had made a friend. *But he knows about Nomad's touch*, he thought. *He sees my strengths, knows some of them . . . how can I take anything for granted?*

He turned away, troubled, and walked towards Reaper.

"Soon," he said as he approached the thing his father had become.

"I hope so," Reaper said.

"Mum always used to like this chain," Jack said, pointing at the shop's name.

Reaper only stared at him, giving nothing away. Then he said, "So, I should go to meet your Irregular friends, don't you think?"

"Just don't kill them all," Jack said coldly.

"What makes you think I would?" Reaper asked.

"You're so good at it."

They didn't have to wait very long.

Jack, Sparky, and Jenna had returned to their table and stood around it, talking in subdued whispers. Reaper and Breezer had faced each other, exchanged a few words, and then parted again. Reaper went back to strolling around the street, sometimes apparently studying his surroundings, at other times engrossed in thought. He seemed unable to stay still for very long. Breezer and the people with him sat along the kerb, two of them smoking, the others passing a bottle of whiskey back and forth. And it was from one of these that the warning came.

"We're being watched," the woman said, standing and squeezing her eyes so tightly closed that her face became a mask of wrinkles.

"Yes," Reaper said.

"No. I don't mean your shadow man. I mean by someone from afar."

"The girl the Choppers have working for them?" Jenna asked.

"Maybe," Jack said. "But . . . I think I hear something."

One by one, they all looked up. A drone buzzed so high up that its sound was a whisper, its shape and form little more than a flash of reflected sunlight.

"Checking us out," Sparky said, giving the thing the finger.

"And when they see who's here, the Choppers won't be far behind."

"Reaper," Jenna said.

"And Jack," Sparky said. "Mate, no risks, huh? That Miller bastard, he was looking at you like he wanted to chop you up."

"Miller won't be chopping anyone else up," Reaper said. He'd drifted closer to them, and now he stood almost as if he was part of the group.

"So what now?" Breezer asked.

"Now we wait," Reaper said. He cocked his head, smiled. "But not for long."

They came four minutes later. Not the royal blue Land Rovers that Jack had seen before, but smaller, faster shapes moving along the streets like errant shadows. They were almost completely silent but for the *whish!* of disturbed air, and the occasional crackling of wheels crunching over grit or litter. He saw six initially, but as he and the others crouched down ready to spring aside, he realised that there were more.

They've sent the whole Chopper army against us! Jack thought, and at that moment the first motorcycle flipped into the air, shed its rider, and smashed into the ground. It bounced and skittered across tarmac and the concrete pavement, slamming into a bank's façade and exploding in a wash of blazing fuel. The sudden sound was shocking, and it spurred everyone into action.

"Into the café!" Jenna shouted, grasping Sparky's hand and waiting for Jack.

Guns fired, bullets ripped along a shop's façade, glass shattered, someone screamed.

Reaper held Jack's arm, and when Jack looked at him the man was smiling. "No need to run," Reaper said.

And he was right. Jack had always counted that Reaper would not be coming on his own, but for the past few minutes he had been worrying that his father was not going to hold up his side of the plan. Shade was there, hiding somewhere out of sight. But Jack had seen no one else from Reaper's retinue.

With the Choppers attacking, they made themselves known.

Several motorcycle wheels exploded into flames and burst, scattering blazing rubber across the street and spilling riders. The bikes flipped over the kerb or collided in the road, and for a few seconds the scene was one of chaotic, deadly movement. Another bike was lifted from the ground and held motionless in mid-air, its rear wheel still spinning frantically, its rider struggling to unsling a machine gun from his shoulder.

Three bikes skidded to a stop along the street and their riders levelled their guns. Jack saw Reaper draw in a huge breath.

"Dad!"

Reaper roared. He was looking at Jack as he did so, but he held nothing back. Shop fronts erupted, paving slabs cracked and shattered, cars immobile for two years slid along the road on flat tyres, and the three motorcycles and riders came apart as the wave of destruction hit them, flesh and metal, blood and plastic merging in a cloud that splashed down along the street and across the front of an old pizza restaurant.

As quickly as it had begun, Reaper's storm ceased. The street held its breath as Superiors emerged from where they had all been hiding. A woman stepped from a rooftop and floated down to the ground, flames playing around her fingertips and at her throat. Her hair seemed to be ablaze, and she looked at Jack with fire in her eyes. Puppeteer stepped from a shop doorway farther along the street, Scryer close behind him. And there were several other, all possessed of a silent, aloof confidence as they claimed the street and the scene of destruction as their own.

Puppeteer held up both hands, and along the street at least eight Choppers were held aloft six feet above the ground. They struggled, but to no avail. One of them shouted as she fought against the hold, struggling to bring her gun to bear, and Jack realised with a sick feeling who was in her sights.

"Jenna, duck!" he shouted. But Sparky had seen at the same time. He shoved his girlfriend aside and fell on her, smothering her with his body and limbs, and Jack thought, *No, Sparky!*

But when the woman's finger squeezed the trigger, it was her own head that the bullet smashed apart. Puppeteer grunted in satisfaction and flicked his hand at the air, sending the woman's corpse crashing against a coffee shop's window and sliding to the pavement. The look of surprise was still etched on her blood-spattered face.

"Don't kill any more!" Jack shouted. "Get them down, take their weapons, but don't kill any more!" He looked over to where Breezer and the other Irregulars were huddled down on the pavement and he couldn't help thinking that this was all going wrong. Brutality was a tool of the Choppers and a weapon of the Superiors, but Breezer and the others did their best to exclude it from their lives.

"Bring them down," Reaper said. His voice was so powerful and held such command that the street itself seemed to be listening.

One of the men with Breezer stood and moved forward. He lowered his head so that he was looking at his feet, and Jack watched, intrigued. Then he said, "Drop your weapons," and there was a clatter of metal on concrete and tarmac as the Choppers all obeyed immediately.

"Nice," Scryer said from where she stood beside Puppeteer. "What do you call yourself?"

"Guy Morris, same as I always have," the man said.

Puppeteer dropped the men and women to the ground. They landed with grunts and cries, quickly stood, and drew together into two groups.

Sparky and Jenna were standing again now, Jenna shaking slightly, Sparky with his arm around her shoulder.

"I've been shot before," she said softly when Jack looked at her.

"I remember," he said.

"It hurt."

"Yeah." Jack looked across at the crumpled Chopper, a pool of blood spreading around her head. "Her fault."

"Precisely," Reaper said. "What these bastards never learn is that we are better than them, and we will win."

Jack's heart thumped, blood pulsing in his ears. He knew that this could turn bad very quickly.

"We won't have long," Sparky said.

"Then let's not waste any more time," Reaper said. He walked closer to one group of Choppers, and two who had discarded their helmets looked at him with unashamed terror.

"No more murdering," Jack said. "We can use them."

"And use them we will," Reaper said. "So. Which one do we interrogate first?"

CHAPTER ELEVEN
HAMPSTEAD HEATH

Each time she blinked, Nomad saw the girl's face. Young, pretty, yet aged with tensions and experiences that were etched into her eyes like memories on view. Her purple hair might have been a bruise. The explosion and the girl were one and the same.

I'm drawing close to her again, Nomad thought. *She's come to the north where the worst of my mistakes live out their lives. The north. I haven't been here for . . .*

After Doomsday, when Nomad found herself wandering the ruined city and becoming something else—drowning in new abilities, and then drowning her past *with* them—she had gone to dwell in the north. It had felt sufficiently different from the rest of London to perhaps allow her some peace. But that peace had failed to manifest, because the north had shown her the worst of what she had done. The monsters had run, crawled, flown, and scampered there, hiding amongst the mazelike streets and parks, and she had wandered amongst them, never touching nor wishing to be touched.

And so Nomad had moved south and found the reality, though that was no less troubling. She had returned north occasionally since then, because her destinations were never purely geographic, and sometimes there was a randomness to her wanderings that made it inevitable. But she had never been comfortable there.

She seeks her brother, but if he is here, she will not want to find him. It was strange thinking of the girl in such terms. Nomad was going to kill her—she was certain of that, convinced, and ready for it—and yet the girl was very real in her mind, with aims and ambitions, fears

and worries. Strange. She did not think of people like that anymore.
Everyone was a ghost to Nomad because she dwelled somewhere so
different.

Everyone but the boy, Jack. *Her* boy. In him she had planted the
seed of her future and hope for redemption. And she would do everything she could to protect him.

"What?" Lucy-Anne asked as she ran. "Rook, *what?*"

"Hampstead Heath," Rook said. "I never thought it would be
so . . ." But she didn't hear what else he said because they were both
running, pounding the pavement, and Rook's birds fluttered around
their heads, their own evident excitement echoing his.

Lucy-Anne had never been to Hampstead Heath before. She was
expecting a park, like any one of London's other large green areas.
What she could not prepare herself for was the sheer scale of the
place. One moment they were running along a residential street,
aiming for a wide junction with shops on the other side of the road.
The next moment, they turned a corner and wilderness confronted
them. A landscape of greenery, much of it strange. A swathe of wild
hillsides, a forest, a jungle of trees and creepers. The shock was
immense, and she was almost winded by it. Then when she breathed
in again she could taste the Heath, and it was both alluring and
terrifying.

"They called it the Lungs of London," Rook said as they jogged.
"So big, it's like a different place. Countryside in the middle of the
city. Sucks in a lot of London's pollution, pumps out oxygen. It did,
at least. Who knows what it pumps out now?"

Lucy-Anne heard but could not respond. At the end of the street
two roads led off, the main one on the left providing what was once
a definitive demarcation point between green and grey. Now, that
line had been blurred. The Heath was spreading, bleeding greenery

from its previously defined borders. The buildings there sprouted grasses, wore climbing plants across their façades, and several seemed to have trees growing through their slated roofs.

Nothing grows that quickly, Lucy-Anne thought. But every sense told her that the Heath no longer obeyed any natural rules she knew. While Evolve had acted upon the human population of London, perhaps here it had also touched the vegetation.

"How the hell are we going to find him in there?" she asked. Rook looked at her, eyes wide with excitement and fear. He could offer her no answer, no comfort. He only took her hand and pulled her along the street.

"The only way is to start looking," he said. "I've sent my rooks ahead. They've been scouting the land while you rested."

"And what have they found?"

"Wilderness. Strangeness. Danger." He smiled at her. "All the usual."

"And nothing to put me off," she said.

"Of course."

They walked on, and Lucy-Anne felt a sudden rush of affection for Rook, and gratitude that he would take it upon himself to do this for her. He was a wild boy himself, and strange, and she knew very well how dangerous he could be. But he was also showing himself to be very human.

"Thank you," she said.

"Haven't found him yet." A bird drifted down to Rook's shoulder, and the dark-haired boy tilted his head. When he did that, Lucy-Anne thought he took on the mannerisms and the look of a rook himself.

"Okay," he said. "We can follow the road onto the Heath. It rises up out of London, and it's pretty overgrown in places. But it looks safe for now."

Lucy-Anne nodded and, hand in hand, they left the London she had once known.

They entered another world.

Walking into Regent's Park had been strange, with its haunting shadows and strange inhabitants. But Lucy-Anne had always maintained the sense of London around her. The city exerted a gravity that had influenced her every step of the way, present in her memories for each step through the park. Here, she felt different. As soon as they moved out of the built-up area and started across the Heath, she was somewhere else. London and everything that had happened was behind her, and ahead lay a future and a place she could not even guess at.

She sensed strangeness all around, but it was with a kind of detachment that she found comforting. The grass was long and sturdy, and it waved with the breeze, forming complex patterns that seemed to speak of something secret. The trees were heavy with shadow, and lush banks of shrubs could have hidden a thousand watchers. But her focus was narrowing now to include her aim and destination, and little else. Andrew smiled in her mind's eye and laughed in her memory. With the toxic city forgotten, it was his gravity that started to draw her in.

The wide path had once been immaculately maintained, with defined edges and its surface kept free of weeds. That had all changed now. They could still follow the route of the tarmac way, because the weeds and grasses that had grown through it were shorter and scrubbier than the surrounding heath. But nature had very definitely taken over here.

They were climbing slowly but surely towards a wide, gentle hilltop. Lucy-Anne glanced occasionally back the way they had come, and each look offered a more comprehensive view across

London. As they approached the crest of the hill she could see Canary Wharf to the left, and to the right the dome of St. Paul's was just distinguishable above the spread of other buildings. Patches of green marked the parks that had grown wild. One tall office building close to the centre of London had been gutted by fire sometime in the past, and now it offered only a fractured skeleton to the sky. Half a dozen smoke trails rose from across the city, leaning to the east like plants erring towards the sun.

"It looks so different even from this far away," she said.

"It's because you know how much it's changed," Rook said. "And there's no sound of civilisation."

Lucy-Anne listened and heard bird song, the howl of something larger, and movement in trees farther along the slope. No cars or sirens or screams of playing children.

A pack of dogs scampered across the slope down from them, and she shivered as she remembered their subterranean encounter with dogs on the way in to London. *I dreamed of them as well*, she thought. She glanced at Rook.

"We need to stay away from the trees," she said.

"Huh?"

"I dreamed of you in there, and then . . ."

He took her hand and kissed her quickly on the lips. "I have my eyes," he said, glancing up. A dozen rooks circled high above them. "Besides, we can't avoid the trees here. You want to look, don't you?"

"Of course."

"Then we have to find someone to help us."

"You're serious?" She thought of the gargoyle people, the snake folk, and other mutations she had been imagining.

"If not, we might be looking forever," he said. "The Heath is almost a thousand acres, and wilder now than ever before. You can feel that?"

Lucy-Anne nodded.

"There must be people among the monsters," Rook said, glancing away from her. "There have to be."

A rush of hopelessness flushed through her, threatening to corrode her determination. But she pressed her lips tight together and clenched her hands into fists.

"I don't care how long it takes," she said. "Come on." She walked uphill, towards a line of trees that marked the end of this open area of Hampstead Heath.

Rook followed, and it was Lucy-Anne who entered the forest first.

They walked for a few minutes, going deeper into the woods and higher up the hillside. Paths crissed and crossed, and she was aware of frequent movement away from them through the trees. They were surrounded by a bubble of stillness and silence. Lucy-Anne had no wish to see what dwelled beyond.

An urge came to start shouting Andrew's name. *He could be close!* she thought, and she walked tall to make herself seen. But she did not shout. She was too cautious for that.

Twenty minutes after entering the woodland, an intense feeling of déjà vu assailed her. She swayed, struggling against the compulsion to slump to the floor and let events wash over her. *Not every dream comes true!* she thought, and she searched among the trees for familiar scenes. There was nothing she recognised.

No bench, no man swinging in the trees, so—

She turned around and Rook was no longer with her.

Lucy-Anne felt her stomach sink, and her heart thumped painfully. Her vision blurred and then settled again, a newfound clarity making everything around her clear, sharp, and deadly.

"Rook!" she called. *He won't answer, he's gone, he's fallen already into the pit just like my dream and—*

"Over here," he said. Lucy-Anne almost collapsed with relief. She took three steps and looked past a big tree, and there he was. He'd run along a shallow gully towards what looked like an old bandstand, and he was now climbing the gully's sides to walk back to her.

There was a bench on the left, halfway between them. Alongside the bench, a coil of green wire, the sort sometimes used in parks to define the edges of a path. On the air, a memory of blackberries.

"No," she breathed. "Rook . . ." But she could not shout.

She tried to close her eyes so that she could not see the man swinging down from one of the trees, but Rook called her name—a shouted warning—and she looked. The man swung between her and Rook, naked and coated with dye, unnaturally long arms heavily muscled . . . directly from her dreams.

"Rook, stop!" she shouted, but he was running. *And now the dog-woman*, she thought, and there she was down the slope, urinating on a tree and sniffing at the ground. "Rook! Don't come any closer!"

"I don't think they mean any—" he began, and then the ground beneath him opened as he ran, swallowing him up as if he was never meant to be there at all. His rooks fluttered and flitted in confusion.

Lucy-Anne's vision began to fade, her world receded, and she bit her lip to try to see away the faint washing over her.

The ape man swung away, the dog-woman scampered into shadows. And from the pit she heard Rook's awful, blood-filled cry.

She staggered to the edge of the pit and looked down. There was Rook. At first she thought her vision was deceiving her, and that it was not a huge, wormlike thing chewing at his throat. A worm-thing with the remnants of humans limbs and long auburn hair.

Noooo, she tried to scream, but it was not even a whisper. The last thing she saw as she hit the ground, rolled, and vision fled was the rooks, hundreds of them spiralling up into the sky and away. She heard their cries, and one more from Rook.

And then nothing.

They are somewhere overgrown, a place where nature has been given back to itself. Humankind has lost dominion here. There is a bench smothered with a rose bush, a path, and—

And this is my dream.

Rook is down the slope from her, moving quickly towards her with a look of excitement. He has seen something that he wants to share. But . . .

But this is my dream, I saw this happening, and soon there will be—

The naked man swings between them from the trees, and this time Lucy-Anne takes time to examine him and the rope he uses. He is smeared with a heavy dye, like coloured mud. Yet he still wears glasses, and she is sure his earrings are the red and yellow of Christmas. The rope is thin and blue, the kind used for tying down loads on the back of trucks. He ends his swing and clambers into a tall tree to her left.

I'm steering this, she thinks. *Already this dream is not progressing like it ever has before.*

She moves forward and looks for the man, but he has scrambled higher into the tree and is hidden from view.

She sees the dog-woman sniffing along at the foot of a tree farther away.

She'll piss, and then Rook will fall into the pit, I'll hear him scream and then look and that horrible worm-thing will be chewing at him, and he'll be dying.

"Rook, wait!" she shouts, and it is the first time she finds her voice.

Rook hesitates, then runs faster towards her.

Not long now. He'll fall.

"Stop running!" she screams. Rook's expression falters, and he skids to a stop twenty feet from her but not far enough away. He slips forward as the ground gives way.

"Grab something! Don't fall! Don't let yourself fall!"

Lucy-Anne is running forwards in her dream, in full control. She feels a gleeful rush of power, and even as Rook is scrabbling for his life she glances to the left. A tree explodes into colour, raining down a thousand fat red blooms that splash across the ground. She looks right and imagines a fully-laid dinner table, and there it is, meats and vegetables steaming all across the crisp white tablecloth.

She screeches in delight, and when she reaches Rook he is hauling himself from the edge of the pit. Something crawls around down there. Something hisses.

"I did it," she says. Rook is silent, almost not there. "I did it." But then she realises that this is a dream, and remembers what she has already seen in real life. She looks sadly at Rook, and he sees his own death reflected in his eyes. He starts to fade away.

There is a jump. Her surroundings change, and though there is no external jolt, inside she feels the shock of displacement. It is a blink between dreams, but Lucy-Anne now knows that she has some say in what she is seeing and experiencing, and that makes the change so much more shocking.

She and Rook are on a wide area of scrubland. London is in the distance so this is still the Heath, but a part of it she has never seen before. It is surreal. A huge table and chair stand before them, fifty times normal size, with long grasses growing around the legs and creeping plants trying to gain the tabletop.

What once were people move across a tree line farther up the hillside. They seem to be crawling on all fours, but she can't quite tell, because there is something so alien about their movements.

So what's this? Lucy-Anne thinks. She urges herself to

wake—actually pinches herself in the dream, feeling the sharp sting of pain—but the dream still has more to show her.

Rook says something she can't quite hear. His voice is distant, and she experiences a moment of complete panic. Perhaps he really is dead, and this dream is simply an unconscious wish.

Of course he's dead! I saw him fall, saw that thing eating at him, so he must be dead, and now—

Nomad appears. She steps from the top of the huge square table and drops to the ground, landing with knees slightly bent and yet seeming to cause and experience no impact. The grasses around her feet barely move.

"You," Lucy-Anne says, fear cooling her blood.

"And you," Nomad says. She looks at Lucy-Anne sadly and raises her hand, and Lucy-Anne senses the staggering amount of power held in Nomad's fist. *Going to blast me scorch me burn me*, she thinks, and between blinks she sees the nuclear explosion that has accompanied every other dream of this woman.

"I'm sorry," Nomad says.

Lucy-Anne steps back. *She's here to kill me!* The scene freezes, filled with potential. "This is my dream," she says aloud, but her voice sounds muffled and contained. "You can't kill me here."

Movement begins again, and everything has changed. Rook is sitting in the long grass, and Nomad is squatting close by, frowning, shaking her head, and looking at Lucy-Anne as if she has seen a ghost.

"But no one knows me," she says.

Lucy-Anne goes to speak, but there the dream ends. Her senses fade back to herself. She feels grass against her cheek, smells the freshly turned mud and foul sewage stench of the pit, and remembers the last time she had really seen Rook.

"Oh, Rook," she said without opening her eyes, and she cried because the dream could not be real.

"It's okay," Rook said. "You fainted. No wonder. That thing stinks."

Lucy-Anne's eyes snapped open and Rook was there, kneeling by her side and resting one cool hand on her brow. He was shaking.

"Thanks," he said. "One more step and I'd have gone right in."

She lifted herself up on one elbow and looked past Rook towards the hole in the ground. The branches that had been laid over it to disguise it stuck up like broken ribs, and from deep in the dark pit she could hear a sickly, wet sound of movement.

"You didn't fall in," she said.

"No. Well, not quite. Almost." Above him his birds were sitting on branches and circling higher above the trees. They seemed calm, watchful.

"But . . ." She did not know what to say, nor how to explain.

"You okay?" he asked. "I mean, you hit the ground hard."

"Yeah, I'm fine. I think."

"Sure? Feeling exhausted, maybe."

"No," she said, shaking her head, shrugging off his hands, standing. She actually felt better than fine. She felt *energised*. "I think I did something," she said.

"We should keep moving." Rook stood protectively close. "I don't like it here."

Of course not, you died down there, Lucy-Anne thought. She started laughing, and Rook looked at her quizzically.

"Huh?"

Lucy-Anne shook her head, and the laughter faded as quickly as it had come.

"You're sure you're okay?" he asked again.

Lucy-Anne pinched herself, hard, but so that Rook could not see. "Yeah. I'm good. So which way?"

CHAPTER TWELVE
INTERROGATION

J ack stood close by Reaper, ready for the interrogation to take place. He wanted to see and hear everything, he wanted to be close to his father, and most of all he wanted to make sure that no one else died.

The surviving Choppers were being kept corralled inside a ruined clothing store, guarded by Shade and a couple of other Superiors, including the blind knife-thrower Jack had seen in action before. They looked nervous but defiant, and Jack wondered whether they were resigned to death. There must have been so much conflict and death in London since Doomsday. He had only been here for a matter of days and he had seen plenty already . . . but there was also the painful idea that he was responsible for much of it.

He hated the thought, but could not shake it. Fleeter had killed those Choppers to protect him. And these scenes now had been initiated by him. He looked at the Choppers huddled in the smashed storefront and tried to convey a sense of calm, but those who looked at him saw nothing of the sort. Fires still burned amongst the crashed motorbikes, and death hung heavy across the street.

"Scryer," Reaper said. "She's all yours." Puppeteer was standing close by, one hand raised slightly, and a female Chopper hung suspended with her feet a metre above the road surface. Her helmet had been ripped off, her blue uniform torn by the impact from when her motorbike had crashed into a pile of café tables and chairs, and an ugly gravel burn covered her left cheek and jawline. Her fear was

obvious, but so were her efforts to hide it. Jack thought she couldn't
have been much older than him.

Scryer stepped forward, glancing at Jack and smirking. But he
could also sense her uncertainty. They had surely tried this before,
and no Chopper had yet revealed the location of Camp H.

"What's your name?" Scryer asked.

"Kerri."

"Where do you come from, Kerri?"

"Ottery, in Devon."

"How many Irregulars have you killed since Doomsday?"

The woman frowned, lips pressed tight as she tried to fight the
urges to speak and tell the truth. She released her breath with a
heavy sigh, and then said, "Two. A man and a . . . a girl . . ." She
looked away from Scryer, across to Breezer and the other three Irregulars waiting by the café. "I didn't mean . . ." she said.

"Where is Camp H?" Scryer asked. Her tone had not changed at
all—calm, mildly inquisitive, almost friendly—but the atmosphere
thickened as soon as she asked the question. Behind him, Jack heard
Jenna whisper something to Sparky, so quiet that he could not make
it out. Reaper shifted position slightly, taking a half step forward.

"I don't know," Kerri said.

"You do know," Scryer said. "And all you have to do is say."

"Puppeteer," Reaper said.

Kerri twitched in the air and screamed as both arms were
tugged above her head. Jack heard a sickening stretching sound, and
the rip of what he hoped was clothing. He grabbed his father's arm
and squeezed.

Reaper looked down at his hand as he might a smear of bird shit
across his coat. But Jack did not let go.

"No more killing," Jack said. "No more torture. Haven't you
tried all this before?"

"Do you think you can tell me—" Reaper began, but Jack delved down, grasped a star, and cut him off with a thought.

I used to love you. It was a silent shout, screamed from his mind into Reaper's. His father's eyes went wide, and for a moment Jack saw the man he used to know. It almost broke his heart.

"Do that again," Reaper said, shaking Jack's hand from his arm. "Just do." The threat was obvious, his voice heavy with potential. One little whisper, Jack knew, and his father could smash him to atoms.

"Breezer," Jack said. "Who did you bring?"

"This is Rika." Breezer touched a woman on the shoulder and muttered something to her. She nodded and then walked across to them, nervous and birdlike in her movements. When she looked at Jack, he had the feeling that she was seeing deep inside him, and she glanced away as if unsettled at what she saw.

"Jack," Jenna said. He turned to his friends, smiled.

"I know," he said.

"Next time they'll send everything." She nodded up at the sky and he looked, already knowing that he'd see the drone again. He stared at it for a while and wondered whose eyes he was looking into at the other end of its reach. Miller's, perhaps. He cruised through the star-scape of his potential, but found nothing that might let him view through the drone's systems. He found that comforting. Having limits made him feel human.

Jack glanced at his father, the Superiors, and the other Irregulars, and knew that he need not mention the urgency here. The air thrummed with it.

The small woman, Rika, reached Scryer and the Chopper woman suspended above the road.

"You'd really like to hold my hand," Scryer said.

"Yes, I would," Rika replied. She held her breath, froze. "Don't do that to me. Don't you *dare* use your talent on me. You carry secrets as much as anyone, and some you wouldn't want revealed." Her voice did not change at all, but the power of her words swung the balance of control. Scryer's smile remained, but it went from natural to pained. Whatever secrets she harboured, she did not wish them shared.

"Her, then," Scryer said, nodding at the Chopper, Kerri.

"Yes," the Irregular woman said. She and Scryer held hands.

"Ask," Rika said.

"Where is Camp H?" Scryer asked.

The Chopper woman shook her head. She was frowning, struggling against Puppeteer's unnatural hold, sweat speckling her face even though there was a cooling breeze. "I . . . I don't . . ."

"You know," Rika growled.

Jack gasped. Her voice had dropped and become much louder, deeper, and beside him he saw Sparky glance at Reaper. But it had not been him. Reaper was smiling with delight, and then Kerri began a long, low whine.

"Don't hurt her," Jenna whispered. But Jack knew that this was now in the hands of Rika and Scryer.

"Keep asking," Rika said, "and I'll go deep."

"Where is Camp H?" Scryer asked again, and again. The Chopper woman shook her head. Rika growled. Some of the observers shifted uncomfortably, and when one of the Choppers shouted in protest, Shade knocked him to the floor.

Kerri's whine did not change, but after a couple of minutes Rika released Scryer's hand and walked back to Breezer, head bowed, her thin form barely casting a shadow.

Puppeteer let Kerri drop. She hit the road and sprawled, and Jenna went to her, kneeling by her side and checking to see how she was. Jack grinned at his friend and her caring nature, and he was proud that she had shown the others how human she was. The woman might be a Chopper, but she was a person as well.

"Well?" Reaper asked, his voice deep. Shattered glass clinked across the pavement, and along the street the flames from the burning motorbikes wafted in the breeze.

Rika whispered to Breezer, and he nodded grimly.

"Breezer," Jack said. "We're all in this together." Breezer glanced from Jack to Reaper, then up at the drone silently circling high up.

"We know," Breezer said. "Camp H isn't really a camp at all. It's located in the centre of a container park."

"A what?" Jack asked.

"Transport containers," Sparky said. "The big metal ones they use to ship stuff overseas. I've seen them stacked five high in yards the size of football fields."

"Bigger," Breezer said.

"They're hidden deep," Rika said. "Confusing even for me to see."

"And you know where it is?" Reaper asked.

"Yes," Breezer said.

Reaper tilted his head and raised an eyebrow. Everyone in the ruined street—Jack and his friends, Irregulars, Superiors, even those Choppers fearing what the immediate future might bring—watched Breezer expectantly.

This is when all the victims of Doomsday form an alliance or go to war, Jack thought, and the others knew that too.

"It's in the Docklands," Breezer said. "A big distribution centre."

Reaper did not smile, but Jack saw a slight relaxing of his shoulders.

"We have to be quick," Jack said. "Element of surprise."

Silence fell over the street. It was a strange silence, one loaded with promise, and Jack felt himself circling the bright points of his talents, both those already known and those he had yet to touch. He felt one step removed from everything.

Reaper gestured across to where Shade was guarding the Choppers. "Get rid of them."

"No!" Jack shouted. From the corner of his eye he saw Breezer and the other Irregulars tense, but none of them came forward. They had nothing with which to stand up to Reaper. "No!" Jack cried again, louder and more determined.

Reaper turned away, not even looking at him.

Not long, not long, I don't have long . . .

Jack closed his eyes, felt through his inner universe, and let a star explode.

In the clothes store where seven Choppers were about to meet their end, a bright light bloomed. It grew and grew, and Shade stood out silhouetted against the light, his arm thrown up and hands pressed against his eyes. The light seemed to bleed through him as if he was not entirely there, and when it began to fade, he slumped to his knees and leaned slowly forward until his forehead touched the ground. Shade had been illuminated.

Reaper turned and started back towards Jack, thunder in his eyes.

"Oh, for *fuck's sake!*" Jenna shouted. She stood beside the fallen Chopper and held up her hands, palms out, in pure despair. "Are you all so *stupid*? This isn't a 'who's got the biggest dick' contest, is it? Jack said it to Breezer—we're all in this together. We've come together and found out something that no one has been able to find out before. Not even you!" She pointed at Reaper then turned her back on him, dismissive. "And the best way to move on from that is . . . what? More murder? More killing?"

"Stay out of this," Puppeteer said, and he raised one hand. Jack tensed, ready to do something, anything, to prevent him from hurting Jenna. But right then he could find nothing. Countless stars were around him, but he floated in the deep spaces in between.

"Oh, grow up," Jenna said.

"That's my girl!" Sparky laughed out loud. "That's my Jenna!"

"Seriously," Jenna said. She looked down at the woman at her feet, then walked across towards the clothing shop. The Choppers there were gathered against one wall, drawn back from where Shade knelt slumped down on the floor. He had yet to look up, but already he was looking less there to Jack. Fading back to the shadows.

"Can't we lock them away somewhere?" Jenna asked. "Or, like . . . freeze them, or something?"

Reaper stood on his own in the middle of the street, expressionless, motionless. Jack knew that he could probably kill every surviving Chopper with one shout. But there was something going on behind his eyes that Jack recognised.

His father was thinking.

"Breezer?" Reaper asked after another few seconds.

Breezer shook his head, shrugged.

"I can do this," Jack said. "Sparky, Jenna, give me a hand. If everyone else can just make sure they don't try anything?"

He and Sparky approached Jenna and the shop, and as they drew close Jack grinned at his friend. She raised an eyebrow and propped a hand on one hip.

"So what are you going to do, Superman?" she asked quietly.

"Just watch."

Ten minutes later they had split into three groups again, after arranging where to meet to execute their assault on Camp H. It had to be quick. It had to be soon. And Jack knew that his mother and sister's lives depended upon whatever plan they all came up with being a success.

"That was pretty cool," Sparky said.

"What, locking them in the basement?" Jack and his friends had ushered the Choppers down into the shop's basement, and Jack had melted the hinges and lock mechanisms of the two sets of doors between them and the staircase. They'd break their way out, given time. But Jack's final words to them, telling them that if they *did* break down the door there would be something waiting for them in the darkness, probably doubled the amount of time they'd stay down there.

They might be Choppers, but they were also people. They valued their lives as much as anyone.

"Huh?" Sparky said. "Oh, that. The doors. Nah, that wasn't cool, that was just heat. I mean *you!*" He leaned into Jenna and slung a hand around her shoulders, and she giggled like a schoolgirl.

"I've got to admit, you're right," Jenna said. "I *was* pretty cool."

They moved quickly, descending from the streets and travelling between Underground stations. Twenty minutes later they were a mile from Covent Garden, and they had an hour to wait until their rendezvous with Breezer and Reaper.

They sat on the old station platform, darkness around them made deeper by the flashlights they'd lifted from a station office. None of them felt like eating, and Jack could not shake the notion that they were wasting time. But they could not risk another confrontation with a larger, heavier-armed troop of Choppers.

Time ticked by, the darkness loomed, and they chatted about lighter, happier times.

"One thing," Jack said to Reaper when they met again that afternoon. "Why did you let Miller live?"

Fleeter accompanied Reaper, and Sparky and Jenna were with Jack, as always. Other small groups of Superiors and Irregulars were moving towards their rendezvous point three miles to the east, from where their assault on the container park would commence. They hoped to leave it to the very last moment before giving away their presence.

Jack had reluctantly admitted that it was Reaper's people who should lead the assault. They were the ones with the most disruptive, destructive powers, and there was no telling how long it would take to find the relevant containers.

"I told you before, he interests me." Reaper and Jack were in the lead, but it could not be said that they walked together. Even if they were shoulder to shoulder, Reaper's dismissive aura would have meant he walked alone.

"It seems like a strange sort of mercy to me," Jack said.

"It's not mercy. I have none for Choppers, and less so for the monster who leads them."

"They why? You had him kneeling before you, defenceless. Yet you let him live, and allowed him to pursue me and my friends."

"I knew he'd never catch you," Reaper said.

"What?"

Reaper glanced over at Jack, and a ghost of something passed from his face, leaving only his brutal expression behind. *What the hell was that?* Jack thought. *It sounded for a moment like he cared.*

"Miller is a man obsessed," Reaper said. "London is his playground, and Irregulars are his test subjects. You know all that. He yearns to get his hands on Superiors, too. See how different *we* are." Reaper tapped his head.

"He's never caught one of yours?"

"Some. They haven't been seen since."

"Probably dead, then," Jack said coldly.

Reaper shrugged as if unconcerned. "As to why I left him alive? London is much more my playground than his. And he is one of my toys. Get rid of Miller, and things around here won't be as . . . exciting."

"You mean that," Jack said. "You really mean it." Reaper walked on ahead and Fleeter followed, walking close to the tall man in black. She touched his arm, slid her hand down, and for the briefest moment they entwined fingers. Then Reaper shook her off, and Fleeter hung back to let him walk ahead.

Jack looked away. That was his father, with another woman. A deep sadness engulfed him, for his mother and Emily, and also because he was not surprised. Reaper projected himself as a heartless, superior man, but he drank whiskey like water, and now it appeared he and Fleeter might be an item. The more Jack saw brief flashes of his father in Reaper's expression and demeanour, the greater the distance seemed between them.

"What about this time?" Jack asked. "Will you kill him now?"

"That's down to Miller," Reaper said without turning around. "It always is."

They walked on, following the course of the Thames. Fleeter flipped now and then to scout their way ahead, and once she told them to change direction and divert around the charred remains of a school. She did not say why, and Jack and his friends did not ask.

Sparky and Jenna walked close to Jack, hand in hand. Their togetherness pleased him, but also made him feel more alone. Jenna could smile and Sparky could give him the finger, but they all knew that things could never be the same again.

Close to East India Dock Road, Reaper called a halt. They entered a hotel through its smashed front door and waited in the reception area while Fleeter did her thing. For several minutes Reaper sat separate from Jack and his two best friends, barely acknowledging their presence. Sparky perused the hotel's guest book, and even when he became quietly excited when he found a rock star's name, Reaper did not react.

Jack sat back in a comfortable chair and closed his eyes. His father was as much an enigma to him now as he was when he'd first clapped eyes on Reaper. Perhaps somewhere deep down he was helping because of Emily and his wife. But perhaps not. If he was not prepared to open up and reveal which, then Jack would have to step away. He'd done all he could to get his father back.

A *clap!* stirred dust across the hotel lobby, and Fleeter sauntered from between two marble columns.

"The Chopper was right," she said. "Half a mile past the Millennium Dome on the north bank. The container yard's massive, but I got in pretty close and saw some of them patrolling."

"You found the containers they're using?" Jack asked.

Fleeter glanced at Reaper. He nodded for her to continue.

"Not as such. But I got close to an open area in the piled containers. A sort of courtyard. I found one route that twisted its way in there, so there'll be others. And there were sharpshooters up on some of the higher boxes."

"How many troops?" Reaper asked.

"Difficult to say. I couldn't get too close, didn't want to risk giving anything away. But I saw at least twenty in the courtyard. Dressed casual, not in Chopper outfits, but they're slack at hiding their weapons."

"Could be countless others in the containers," Jenna said.

"Yeah, great place for a barracks," Sparky said.

"Tell the others," Reaper said.

"Hang on a minute." Sparky walked from behind the reception desk, twirling a set of keys on one finger. "We can't just storm in all gung-ho."

"I don't storm anywhere," Fleeter said.

"You're as good as a blazing gun," Jenna said. "All you Superiors are. No subtlety, that's your problem. So, we go in like that and they'll respond in kind. Who's to say they won't just execute whatever prisoners they have and then get away somehow? No way they'd risk an HQ like this without having a pretty good escape plan. In case of . . ." She waved her hand at Reaper.

"In case of something like this," Sparky said.

"So what do you suggest?" Reaper asked.

"The girl," Jenna said. She glanced around at them all, and her gaze finally rested on Jack.

"Yeah," Jack said. "Show of strength." He glanced at Fleeter. She was smiling at him, leaning against a wall, hand on hip. She was trying to look seductive, and after what he'd seen her do he found that grotesque. But they could work together.

"You and me?" Fleeter asked.

Jack nodded.

"We go in, kill the girl, show them they don't have a hope." Fleeter's voice was high with excitement.

"No!" Jenna said. "Don't you get it, you stupid bitch? You don't kill her. You don't kill anyone. You just—"

A *clap!*, a swish of air across the hotel lobby, and between blinks Fleeter was behind Jenna with one arm tugging across her neck. Jenna gasped in surprise, then choked, clawing at Fleeter's arm. But the woman was stronger than she looked.

Sparky threw a punch and Fleeter stepped aside, dodging the blow without having to flip.

"Stop it," Jack said, but no one heard. He glanced at his father, breathed deeply, and spoke the words again, this time imbuing them with Reaper's power.

Behind the counter, cobwebbed keys jangled on their hooks, and dust rose from the lobby carpet. The building itself seemed to grumble, and everyone froze.

With a grunt, Jenna shoved Fleeter away. Sparky glared at the woman, and Reaper watched them all with a humourless smile.

"What Jenna said," Jack said. "We don't kill anyone. We need a distraction, then Fleeter and I go in and take the girl. Bring her out. Show them what we can do right under their noses, and that to stand against us will be hopeless."

"Even if there's forty of them?" Sparky said. "Eighty? A hundred?"

"They're ants," Reaper said.

"Ants with machine guns!"

"We'll force a stalemate," Jack said. "They've got a perfect hiding place, but it'll go against them as well. They might know the area, but they can't see around corners."

"And you can?" Breezer asked.

Jack shrugged. He hadn't tried. "With the talents we have here, we can find our way in. And it's the best way. If what we're doing here is actually going to help anyone, we have to move on. Them picking up Irregulars and hunting for . . ." He nodded at Reaper and Fleeter. "And you killing them whenever you can. If any sort of progress is to be made, the killing has to stop. Here and now."

"Progress," Reaper said slowly, as if tasting the word.

"I'll be your distraction," Sparky said.

"Me too." Jenna turned her back on Fleeter and faced Jack. "And maybe Breezer and a couple of his people can help."

Reaper grunted in agreement.

Jack experienced a sudden, overwhelming sense of familiarity—the way his father stood with his hands behind his back, the brush of his hair, the shadow of weak light falling across his cheek and chin. He wanted to go to him and hug him, squeeze away the last two years and tell him how much he loved him, and how much they all needed him.

"And if the distraction fails," Reaper said, "we'll be waiting to mop up the pieces."

"It won't fail," Jack said. But the fragility of their alliance was already obvious. Reaper and his people seemed almost flippant in their confidence, and there was no telling what their real aims and ambitions were. Reaper had left Miller alive because he amused him. Like a cat leaving a mouse to play with the next day.

And yet Jack was certain that there were underlying insecurities that he had yet to find. If not, why did Reaper not rule London?

And why was he even still here?

He sighed, and thought of his mother and Emily.

They slowly drew together with the others. One of the women with Breezer could communicate in a basic way with her mind, sending hints and urges rather than words. She liaised their meeting point, and long before they got there, Jack and his friends saw the huge area of stacked containers.

It was almost beautiful. The rectangular metal containers came in an array of colours—yellow, green, rusty red, cream, varying shades of blue. There seemed to be no design to how they were stacked, and the mess of colours was busy and pleasing to the eye. But knowing what lay within the container park gave it a sinister edge.

This was where Miller and his Choppers operated from. A place of imprisonment and cruelty. A place of chopping to see what made London's survivors—the New—able to do the amazing things they could. He probed inward and reached out, but he was not able to see far into the maze of containers. It was confused. He wasn't sure why, but his senses were flooded with input from all around, like splashes of colour and light on a dark background. Thousands of containers filled with millions of items. Perhaps they all meant something to someone—all bearing distinct, deep histories—and that concentration of meaning was confusing his talents.

They crossed a wide spread of concrete and approached the first of the containers, watching out for movement. Breezer and his people emerged from behind one of the metal boxes where they had been waiting, and without a word they joined forces. It was a significant moment, marked by no more than a glance between Reaper and Breezer. Both men hid their thoughts.

The Choppers already knew they were there. Of course they did. They had the girl working for them. But this time the advantage belonged to the New.

Jack and Fleeter held back at the tail end of the group as they moved into a shadowy passageway between container piles. The route quickly became as wide as one of London's streets—wide enough for container trucks and mobile cranes, Jack guessed. Sparky and Jenna led, with Breezer and the three Irregulars just behind them. Puppeteer followed, to the side and slightly apart. Reaper had vanished, advancing from elsewhere, and Jack knew that others would be with him—Shade, Scryer, and more.

So these are the New, Jack thought, and a tingle ran down his spine. Tense though this moment was, it was also painfully exciting. He had seen more death and murder than anyone his age should ever see, and he hoped that this might be the first step beyond that.

But he also knew that grudges ran white-hot. The slightest mistake could push one side or the other over the precipice.

After ten minutes wending their way between piled metal containers, Fleeter grabbed his arm and pulled him close. The others paused as well, watching expectantly.

"The open area is around the next junction," she said, nodding at where two routes met a hundred yards ahead.

"The air's loaded," Jack said. "Tense."

"Don't need Spidey senses to feel that," Sparky muttered.

"They'll have guards," Jenna said.

"And the sharpshooters I told you about," Fleeter whispered, pointing up.

"Come on," Jack said. "Fleeter and I will get out of sight while you move on. But . . ."

"Of course we'll be careful," Sparky said

Jenna nodded. "I'll look after him."

Jack watched his friends moving away from him, and the sinking feeling could only have been dread.

Fleeter grabbed his hand and pulled, edging into a much narrower gap. Then she started to climb. He followed, glancing up and then looking away, embarrassed, when he realised he could see up her short skirt. He heard her chuckling above him, and he concentrated on handholds and footholds. In places it was easy, and elsewhere he had to prop himself across the gap and edge upwards an inch at a time. After a few minutes Fleeter's hand reached down and helped haul him up, and they emerged into sunlight.

Jack rolled onto his stomach and looked around. They'd climbed four containers, and around them many were stacked only two or three high. Fleeter pressed her finger to her lips and pointed, and thirty yards away Jack could see someone lying on a lower box, rifle resting before them. They had one hand pressed to their ear, listening to some sort of communicator. Binoculars sat beside them. Fleeter gesticulated "wanker," then nodded in the opposite direction. To the east the wide, open area where there were no units at all was obvious. They crawled across the roof of the container, keeping as low as possible, and looked down onto a large expanse of concrete.

There were several Chopper vehicles parked there, Land Rovers and a few of the powerful motorbikes they'd seen only recently. People rushed around, weapons on display. They exuded an aura of confidence. *Good*, Jack thought. *We'll soon change that*.

Fleeter tapped his arm and pointed. Across the other side of the open area, which must have been the size of a football pitch, several metal containers seemed somehow out of place. They'd been placed side to side in two distinct arrangements, one consisting of four units, the other three. Electrical cable was strung around them, and around them were the signs of a well-used compound. Oil drums were stacked beside one, pallets held plastic containers of food and water. Spare tyres, a row of portable toilets, stacked bags of rubbish, and there were even several large, open tents.

They're settled, Jack thought. *Safe. At ease.* He could not hold back the smile. And then from below, a shouted warning.

"Stop right there!" Across the clearing, men and women brought up their weapons and pointed them at the intruders. Some of them edged sideways until they aimed from behind vehicles. Others went to their knees, rifles propped against shoulders.

Sparky, Jenna, and the others had emerged from the maze of containers and now stood at the edge of the open area. Breezer glanced back, and Jack realised for the first time how nervous the man was. He'd spent the past two years trying to avoid Choppers. Now he was offering himself to them, in full knowledge of what they did.

"Stay strong, not long now," Jack muttered. Beside him, Fleeter giggled. He ignored her.

The man next to Breezer lowered his head and looked at his feet, and Jack just caught his words. "Drop your weapons."

From across Camp H, the clatter and clash of guns being dropped.

"That's us," Jack said, turning to Fleeter. She raised an eyebrow at him, licked her lips as she looked him up and down, and then vanished with a *crack!* and a swirl of dust.

Jack concentrated, grasped the talent, and did the same.

CHAPTER THIRTEEN
OTHER MONSTERS

"You don't seem surprised," Rook said.

"Seen it before."

"On TV or something, yeah?"

Lucy-Anne shook her head. Rook frowned, but said no more.

The sculpture was huge, outlandish, and it seemed even stranger now that there was no one left to appreciate it. The table was thirty feet tall, plain, square-edged. An equally plain chair was tucked halfway beneath it, and together they dwarfed the landscape. Lucy-Anne couldn't shake the unsettling conviction that she, Rook, and the surroundings were too small, rather than the table and chair being too large. It was dizzying and unreal, but she was not too concerned with what she saw now.

It was what might come next that concerned her.

"Nomad's here," she said. Farther up the slope, shadows moved slowly uphill.

"So did you dream that as well?" Rook's voice was loaded with doubt, and she looked at the boy who was barely older than her, his dark beauty belying the dreadful things he was capable of. *I saw him having his face eaten off*, she thought, but already she could not recall whether that had been a dream and what came after was real, or the other way around. Had she really dreamed to re-imagine reality? Or had reality merely followed the course of her dream?

"I'm so glad you're alive," she said, realising how strange that must sound to him. She hadn't told him. How could she? *The worm monster ate you, but I dreamed it all differently and now you're not dead.*

"You're strange," Rook said. For an instant his voice sounded almost childish—as it should sound coming from a boy his age, when adulthood and childhood still crossed paths—and Lucy-Anne laughed out loud. A killer and an innocent, perhaps Rook was no longer capable of subtleties of emotion.

At the edge of the tall tabletop, a silhouette shifted.

"There," Lucy-Anne breathed, laughter ceasing.

"Oh," Rook breathed.

Nomad stepped from the table and fell softly to the ground, landing on her feet without causing an impact. Lucy-Anne wondered whether the grass even bent beneath her feet. She looked like a special effect, superimposed on the strange reality of London without any influence on the surroundings. *It's like she's too real and everything else is a shadow*, Lucy-Anne thought, and the idea disturbed her terribly.

"Is that you?" Rook asked.

"What do you mean?"

"You. Is that you doing that?" He was looking at Lucy-Anne, not at Nomad. Denying her presence, not wishing to see her.

"No," Lucy-Anne said. "Who do you think I am?"

"I don't . . ." Rook said. He was confused and vulnerable. She didn't like him like this. Not one bit.

Nomad was watching them. Her hair shifted to an absent breeze, her clothes were old and tattered and yet suited her perfectly. Her eyes were piercing. She might have been mad, or scared.

"You," Lucy-Anne said. *She came to kill me, but that was before my dream. Or is this my dream?*

"And you," Nomad said. She started walking forward, raising her fisted hand as if ready to open it palm-up, presenting something for Lucy-Anne's perusal. But this was death she brought with her. She could scorch Lucy-Anne to a cinder with a gasp, blast her apart with a blink, crush her into a smear across the wild landscape with one stamp of her boot.

"I'm sorry," Nomad said, and the wretchedness did not sit well with her strength.

But things had already changed.

"I dreamed of you," Lucy-Anne said, "and you won't kill me here."

The woman frowned, then—

—she opened her hand. But everything had suddenly changed. The power she had been nurturing in her fist ready to blast the girl and her bird-boy to nothing but memory had become something else; a swarm of flies, flitting to the air and dispersing from view. And Nomad was glad.

The fear she had felt whenever she thought or dreamed of the girl had changed into a stunned fascination. And she was pleased.

The girl has *to die*, she thought. She closed her eyes briefly and recalled the visions from her dream—the mushroom cloud, the blast-wave levelling what was left of London, and her boy Jack meeting his end before he had even touched a fraction of his potential.

She felt herself steered towards other actions. She experienced a flush of déjà vu, as if she had dreamed this same scene a thousand times. *Now I walk forward and squat in the grass, the boy cannot accept me because I trouble him so, but the girl talks to me. We exchange information, discuss plans. We are like friends.* Yet she had never dreamed of this meeting before. Not like this, and not with this result. The girl had been a horror in her imagination, but now she was rapidly becoming something else.

Nomad lowered her hand and walked towards the girl. She was confused, frowning. Shaking her head. *I am my own woman*, she thought, but the startling déjà vu remained. She grasped onto it for as long as she could, because for the first time in years Nomad did not feel responsible. She was not master of her own actions, and she could allow a small weight, at least, to lift from her shoulders.

In that moment of clarity she understood that her guilt would have killed most people, but she had borne it with madness. Perhaps because she sought a way to put everything right.

Maybe she *is the way.*

"But no one knows me," Nomad said.

"It doesn't matter," the girl said. "My name is Lucy-Anne, and I think you can help."

Nomad went to her knees and ran her hands through the long grass, really connecting with the world. Heat grew behind her face. For the first time since she had become Nomad, she began to cry.

Rook stayed close to Lucy-Anne for a few more moments. She could hear his heavy breathing, sense his fear, and when he reached for her hand she took it and squeezed. His rooks were circling high above, and many had landed in the tree bordering this open land to the north. She had never seen them so far away from him.

"I need to . . ." Rook said. He let go and turned his back on the woman, retreating a dozen steps before sitting down and looking out over London.

"He doesn't believe in me," Nomad said. Her voice was smooth, authoritative, even though Lucy-Anne had seen the glimmer of tears.

"I'm sure he does, otherwise he wouldn't be scared."

"I saw you," Nomad said. "In dreams." There was more, but the beautiful, terrifying woman frowned and fell silent.

"Me too," Lucy-Anne said. "And every time I saw you, the world blew up."

"Yes," Nomad breathed.

Lucy-Anne went almost close enough to touch and then kneeled before her. They breathed the same air. She could smell fire and death, and the scent of London turned to dust. But she could not be afraid.

"I don't know if this changes anything," Lucy-Anne said. "Don't know if I can alter something that big."

"Alter?"

"In my dreams." Lucy-Anne blinked and caught a brief, terrifying image of the world behind and around Nomad aflame, rolling waves of fire and destruction sweeping across Hampstead Heath and reducing the weird sculpture behind her to splinters, and ash.

"You're very special too," Nomad said.

"That's why you came to kill me?"

"I came to . . . I did. But no more."

"It's bigger than us both," Lucy-Anne said. "But where does it come from? What is it? Is that their final way of getting rid of their London problem forever?"

"It's *my* London problem."

"Don't kid yourself. While you wander around being all new-age, the Choppers are using everyone and everything. Maybe the bomb . . . maybe it's what happens when they've nothing left to find out."

"They'll always have more to find out," Nomad said, voice strong with certainty. "They've barely scratched the surface."

"Maybe they've scratched it and not liked what they've found."

"And you," Nomad said, looking her up and down. "What about you? Came in from outside. Weren't here. Untouched by my Evolve."

"I've always had strange dreams," Lucy-Anne said. "Since coming into London, they've been growing stronger."

"You're in a place where you don't have to hold back anymore," Nomad said.

"I've never held back. Not consciously. Just . . . never really understood."

"You've been scared of what you can do. Now you're not so scared anymore. You're . . ." She leaned forward, breathing in as if smelling Lucy-Anne. "You're amazing. Everything I wanted to find, before this. Everything I wanted people to be. I knew you were out there, and those like you. With Evolve, I wanted to change everyone."

"Without even asking them if you could."

Nomad glanced away, perhaps distracted, perhaps shamed.

"I saw someone living in a pit in the ground, like a giant worm. A dog-woman pissing against a tree. And there must be others."

"Other monsters, and so many dead."

She carries such weight. Lucy-Anne could hardly question the woman's madness, because how else could she cope with the scope of what she had done?

But this was not about Nomad.

"I'm looking for my brother. Andrew. I've been told he's here on the Heath, and I need to find him. He's all I have left."

"All? What about . . . ?" Nomad pointed to Lucy-Anne's head, waved a hand around her own.

"The things we see?" Lucy-Anne asked. "They're just . . . things we see. Not all dreams come true."

"But this one is dreamed by us both."

Yes, she thought. *I wish I could change my dreams.*

"Please help me find Andrew. He'll be my strength. Then together, maybe we can find out what it means."

"I'll do everything I can to stop it," Nomad said. "Everything. I have to make amends, and my London needs to remain for me to do so."

"Your London?"

They stared at each other for a while, both strong and determined, both troubled by visions neither of them really understood.

"Andrew," Nomad said. "Let me see him." She reached forward for Lucy-Anne's face, fingers splayed.

"You'll find him?"

Nomad touched her. Lucy-Anne felt a rush of memories of Andrew, from when they were younger all the way to the last time she had seen him. They fought and argued and loved like brother and sister, and her tears came strong and unbidden.

"I've *found* him," Nomad said. She stood, turned, and before Lucy-Anne could say any more, she was gone.

Nomad ran. Flowed. Drifted. London moved beneath her, and she crossed the Heath like a memory.

Lucy-Anne's brother was a warm point in her mind; a collection of senses and echoes, a smear of colour, a splash of light. She was already closing in on him, and knew that he would be easy to find. Of course. She was Nomad.

As she moved, it began to feel like something fundamental about her had changed. In the girl, she had encountered something she did not understand, a talent she could not ascribe to the Evolve she had released across London. *I went to kill her and came away her friend*, Nomad thought. Though inexplicable, that was something that pleased her. But the change seemed deeper, and she extended her awareness to analyse it.

All around, the monsters moved. She saw them and felt them, and sensed how troubled they had suddenly become. *What's this?* she thought. She passed a gathering of shadows hiding beneath a copse of trees, and though they watched her, she was not the cause of their turmoil. There was something else, deeper.

They are not such monsters, she thought. And it came as a shock.

Something else she had learned today, another surprise, and Nomad felt suddenly more human than she had for some time. There were things she did not know. Assumptions she had made. She slowed her run and spread her perception, and beneath the wild veneer she discovered a world of complexity and intelligence surrounding her, and echoes of continuing agony at the radical changes that were still taking place. *Not such monsters at all.*

She wanted to stop and examine. Their minds were suddenly deep and expansive, their thoughts and aims open to view, as if she had broken through the crust of their monstrousness to discover endless potential beneath.

Even Nomad, it seemed, was guilty of preconception.

But she did not have the time. Their true natures were open to her because something troubled them deeply, and their defences—that crust of camouflage—were down. They ebbed and flowed across the Heath, and she passed through the tides of their discontent, closing on the sharp image of the girl's brother. He suddenly seemed so very important, and this all felt connected.

"Everything is changing," Nomad said. Something called out loud in agreement. Another voice added a growl. She saw the source of neither, and did not seek them out.

Soon, Andrew was close. She closed on a dilapidated folly tower on top of a gentle rise, and though the door had been bricked up decades ago, she knew that he was inside.

"Andrew," she said, standing at the foot of the tower.

Andrew emerged from the folly. He stepped through the solid stone blocks filling the doorway and dropped gently to the ground.

"You're dead," she said, wondering how this could be. Nomad had been a scientist, and she had never believed in ghosts.

"No," he said. "I dreamed that I would never die. Who are you?"

"So you're a ghost. I'm Nomad."

"I've heard of you. And I don't think there's a name for what I am. My dream keeps me alive, and everything I was, apart from my body, persists here."

"Where is that body?"

"Gone."

"Lucy-Anne looks for you."

He glanced away.

"She thinks you're still alive. She says you're all she has left. Your parents are dead."

Andrew blinked at something out of sight.

"You should come with me. Talk to her."

He looked back at her, faded eyes flickering, but remained silent.

Nomad sighed, deciding to change tack. "What were you doing in there?"

"Hiding. Why aren't you hiding too?"

"Why should I hide?"

"Because the end is close." He walked down closer to her, and she could almost see through him. "Surely you of all people can feel it?" he asked.

"Tell me, Andrew."

"If you promise not to tell her about me," he said. "I don't want her to know me like this. Lucy-Anne. Lucy-Anne." He seemed sad as he tried her name, perhaps for the first time in years.

"I promise," Nomad said. "Though perhaps she will dream the truth from me."

He pointed down at a fallen stone across the hillside. "I crawled there. Among my remains you'll find . . . something to give her. My sweet sister."

Then he closed his eyes and told her the terrible truth.

CHAPTER FOURTEEN
OUT WITH THE OLD

It took Jack a few moments to gather himself. Dust motes hung in the air and the sound of his breathing seemed echoless, lifeless. Even the taint of Nomad in his mouth seemed old and strangely lifeless. Then he crawled to the edge of the stack of three containers and scrambled carefully to the ground.

Around the corner, he saw Fleeter already running past Sparky and the others.

"Wait!" Jack called, but it was like shouting underwater. So he ran instead, only glancing at his two frozen friends as he dashed by. Jenna's eyes were half-closed in a slow, long blink, and Sparky's were turned to the left, looking right at Jack. *He knows I'll be passing by*, Jack thought. It was strange, feeling his friend's eyes upon him yet knowing he could not see. Of all the powers Jack had tapped into, this was the most staggering. He felt a moment of awed terror at what he was doing, and an intense, shattering certainty that all this was very, very wrong. But he could not stop now.

Everything depended on the next few moments.

Jack caught up with Fleeter as she paused by one of the Chopper vehicles. He grabbed her arm tightly, and when she looked back she was grinning, looking down at his hand with eyes wide, excited. He wondered whether she had done anything other than murder during her slowed-down existence, then shook the idea away.

"You're slow," she said. "Come on. Not long."

"We've got—"

"Got to be quick," she finished for him. She nodded back at Sparky and the others. "They might only have seconds."

"But the Choppers have dropped their weapons." And it was true. The soldiers all looked confused and shaken, probably in the middle of wondering why they had suddenly dropped their machine guns.

"Not all of them," Fleeter said. "Only the ones he could see." She nodded up at the surrounding piled containers where they had seen a sniper, and where more might be hiding.

They ran. Across the rough concrete, past the Land Rovers and two vans, and as they approached the larger of the container arrangements Jack had a sudden pang of terror. What would they find inside? He hoped his mother and Emily. But he could not help fearing the worst.

Fleeter paused by a couple of wooden boxes that had been laid to form steps.

"What?" Jack asked.

"Door," she said, pointing up. The side of the container was swathed in canvas, but a sheet of it was pinned aside, showing the gleaming bottom third of a metal doorway formed in the unit's wall. "More than meets the eye."

"You can open it?" he asked.

"Dunno. You got a special finger-shaped-like-a-key power, Jack?"

Jack ignored her and stepped up to the door, shifting the canvas aside and searching for a handle. He found it, pushed down, and was surprised when the door clicked open.

"Oh, that's careless," Fleeter whispered. She climbed the boxes to stand close beside him. "We won't have long. Opening the door will cause a storm inside at their speed, because the pressures will rapidly change. Then they'll just start shooting." Fleeter's previous flippancy had vanished and now she was all seriousness. Jack should have been pleased. But the shock of what was revealed as Jack hauled the door open excluded anything else

The connected units still formed several compartments, with a corridor running along one side. They were staring now into the corridor and the first compartment, and it was an operating theatre. At least that was what Jack thought at first. But closer examination revealed greater, more terrible detail, and it was only Fleeter's hand against his back that prevented him from tumbling back down the impromptu steps.

Oh no, oh no, oh no, he thought, and the terror of what he saw conjured images that strove to still his heart and steal every ounce of determination and resolve he had. Operating theatres were clean, caring places, their sterile atmospheres filled with good intentions and positive thoughts. There might be blood, but it was quickly mopped up. There would be tools that looked severe and even grotesque, but they would be perfectly, caringly manufactured to make lives better. Not to take lives. Not to torture.

The operating table was a slab of metal with a drainage channel around all four sides, pipes venting into several large plastic containers beneath the table. They were opaque, but Jack could still see that they were half-filled with a dark fluid. Blood also still smeared the table and was splashed across the floor, drying in boot-print patterns. Along the far wall was a metal counter propped on thin legs, and it was scattered with an array of tools. He could make out several saws of varying sizes, heavy knives, scalpels, and a couple of chunky devices with thick springs and wide clamps. Other were beyond identifying. Some of the tools looked all too familiar from his father's work shed at home, and the room took another leap away from being an operating theatre. This was a dissection suite.

A man dressed in jeans and a canvas jacket was bent over by the head of the table. He was picking something up from the floor and depositing it in a bag, the bag already bulging with other things. He was almost motionless, and the slowness of his movement—as invisible as the shifting minute hand of a clock—gave the scene a strangely fluid property.

Other things in the bag, Jack thought, still struggling to comprehend the awfulness of this, and some of those things could have belonged to Emily or his mother. Because as he stepped inside to get a better view of the torture chamber, he could see the pink fleshiness of the object in the man's hand.

"We should kill him," Fleeter breathed, and Jack wanted to, more than anything else right then—more than rescuing his family, if they were still alive; more than doing something good and strong that might help London's survivors find a safer, calmer future—he wanted to kill this man. But as Fleeter crossed the room, stepping over blood and moving more gracefully than Jack had yet seen, reality hit home.

"Fleeter," he said, his voice deadened by whatever enabled them to do this. "The girl."

Jack turned from that awful room and walked along the corridor. It ran the length of the four containers, and he could see three more doors leading off to the right into other, smaller rooms, as well as one at the end. There was also a woman in the corridor. She was pushing her glasses up onto the bridge of her nose, her other hand resting on the door handle closest to Jack as she prepared to enter.

And see what? he thought, heart racing. *What are these bastards doing here?* But he knew very well. This was vivisection.

He planted his hand on the woman's chest and shoved her aside. She felt strange to the touch, her chest almost solid, yet not quite mannequin-hard. Her expression did not alter, but as she bounded from the wall and slid along the floor the effect of the impact was dreadful. Her right arm was crushed slowly, violently around her body, shoulder popping, and as her hand glanced from her face her nails opened ugly gashes across her nose and over her forehead. Even though in Jack's view she moved normally, in her reality the impact would have been impossibly rapid and brutal. He hoped he had not killed her. But he didn't care enough to check.

Fleeter was behind him as he shoved the handle down on the metal door and shoved it open.

It was a store room. All four walls of the container were lined with shelving, and eighty percent of the shelves contained glass sample jars. They were strapped in for safety. Their contents were not easily identifiable.

"Bastards," Fleeter said.

"How many people?" Jack wondered. There must have been two hundred jars there. "How can they . . . ?"

"What, justify this?"

Jack nodded, but he already knew the answer. "They don't have to," he said. "As far as the world knows, London is filled with monsters."

"Camp H certainly is," Fleeter said. "Come on. The girl."

They stepped over the woman sprawled in the corridor—her expression changing infinitely slowly from mildly distracted, to shocked and agonised—and kicked open the next door. The room was filled with equipment, tools, and a heavily stocked weapon rack. Fleeter grabbed a pistol and several magazines and offered them to Jack, but he shook his head. She raised an eyebrow.

"It wasn't an invitation," she said.

Jack took the gun. She pointed briefly at the switch above the trigger. "Safety. And there's one in the handle, squeeze that when you're shooting."

The next room was a bathroom, and then the corridor ended

with another door. Fleeter went to kick it open but Jack held up his hand, one finger raised.

He half-closed his eyes and cruised his star-scape of potential, realising even as he tried that he had yet to employ one talent whilst already using another. His awareness of Fleeter and his surroundings diminished, and he probed outwards, projecting his senses through the metal door and into the room beyond. There were three warm sensations in there. Jack closed in and merged his own senses with the first—

He smells coffee, thick and bitter; hears a long, low moan, and realises it is someone else in mid-sentence, their words slowed to an impossible crawl; sees two women across from him, one of them biting into a bar of chocolate, the other open-mouthed as she speaks, both cradling guns across their laps, the room lined with computers and wheeled chairs, a map on one wall, screens buzzing mid-flash. And in that other person's mind which is more alien than Jack could have possibly imagined, a frozen image of what its owner would rather be doing right now. The stilled thought includes both women across from him.

Jack notices the grille in the wall behind the women, then, and the shadow outlined beyond. There is a weak light in that smaller room. When Jack shifts his perception he touches upon an incredible, tortured mind, and the pain within is—

—Jack pulled back through the door to himself, shivering as he reined in his senses. He panted heavily, rubbing his hands across his eyes as if that might clear him of another person's distress and wretchedness.

"What?" Fleeter asked.

"Horrible," Jack said. "The poor girl, the poor . . ."

Fleeter shoved him against the door. "What?"

"Three Choppers. Control room. The girl's in a smaller room . . . a cell . . . and she's—"

Fleeter slammed the handle down and entered the room. Jack went to follow but slumped against the cold doorframe, watching helplessly as Fleeter shoved the two women aside. When they struck the desks and floor, blood flowed. She tried the door but it was locked and bolted. When she glanced back at Jack, he was already moving towards her.

"Stand back." He concentrated, and the two heavy hinges glowed red, white, then dripped and melted. Fleeter pulled the door again, and sweat flushed down Jack's face as he concentrated some more. Then the door squealed open, molten metal pattering across the floor. Smoke hung lazily in the air.

And Jack saw the girl, who was no girl at all. She must have been eighteen. Pretty once, perhaps, now she was restrained by ropes tied around her arms and legs, her emaciated body wrapped in shapeless clothing, dark hair knotted and dirty. A waste bucket sat beneath her seat, and it was the indignity of this more than anything that stirred Jack's rage. He'd seen body parts and blood, jars filled with dissected brains and other organs, and the evidence of the slaughter carried out here in the name of science—or perhaps simply in the name of fear and hate—was incontrovertible. But seeing this poor girl and the bucket she had to piss in brought it all home.

"Bastards!" he shouted. Fleeter glanced at him, her usual manic grin absent. She pulled a flick-knife from her pocket and sliced through the ropes. Then she lifted a thinner strand and held it up for him to see.

"What?" Jack asked.

"Drugging her."

"Cut it."

Fleeter did so, and as the girl slumped slowly onto her seat, the pipe started to swing away, dripping a hazy fluid across the floor. She moved to her own time, and Jack had plenty of time to catch her before she fell.

"Won't it kill her moving her at our speed?" he asked. "She doesn't have what we have."

"It'll hurt her," Fleeter said. "But we need to get her back through there. Just be careful not to bump her against anything."

Jack glanced behind at the three guards. Fleeter had shoved them all aside, and now they sprawled on the floor, still gradually shifting from the staggering impacts her contact had subjected them to. Maybe they were dead; right then, Jack did not care. He hated them enough to kill them himself, but every second they had was precious.

"Give me a moment, then bring her," Fleeter said. Her voice had grown serious, and in her eyes Jack saw his own rage reflected. At the sight of the girl she'd lost some of her aimless anger, and now her fury was defined.

"Fleeter . . ." But she was gone, across the room and out into the corridor. He could have called her back. Could have prevented her from doing what he knew she was about to do. But his own fury held his voice, and as he lifted the poor girl into his arms he heard a sound like paper tearing.

Fleeter was waiting for him back at the door into the container. Jack only glanced into the torture room, and barely winced slightly at the sight of the man and his slashed throat. She'd used the same knife that had freed the girl, and there was some justice in that. But Jack was also unsettled that the sight of murder troubled him so little.

The girl was light, emaciated, hungry, and might well have been dead. But he could sense her life, and something about it was unbelievably strong. Without even trying—without clasping a talent—he could tell that she was alive, and furious, and that he would get to know her well. That was not some prescient thought, but a silent vow.

"They must be keeping my mother and sister in the other containers," Jack said as he followed Fleeter down the boxy steps.

"If they're not dead already."

"We have to look."

The scene was much as they had left it . . . but not *quite*. The Choppers across Camp H were all backing away, confused at whatever had compelled them to drop their weapons. Beyond, Sparky and Jenna had taken half a step forward, and Breezer, the Irregulars, and Puppeteer were all advancing as well.

Fleeter glanced across at the other conjoined containers, then up behind Jack. "Out of time," she said, pointing.

From atop a stack, something was growing. Jack frowned, squinting against the light. Even the sunlight felt slow.

"What's that?" he asked.

"They've started shooting," Fleeter said.

"Shit."

"We've got maybe a minute before—"

"You go," Jack said, nodding down at the girl in his arms. "And take her with you." He was now more convinced than ever that the other three containers formed a prison. A cattle truck, where they kept the subjects for their gruesome, inhuman experiments.

"You really want to play a lottery for whom that bullet's aimed at?" Fleeter said. She was pointing up, and Jack could now see a metallic smear to the air ahead of where the flash of gunfire and smoke was blooming from high up. *I'm watching a bullet travel through the air*, he thought, amazed. It was just about the only thing visibly moving.

Neither of them knew whom the shooter had been aiming at.

"Damn it."

They hurried back across the clearing towards their friends and allies, and as they reached them Jack saw a smear of blood hazing the air around the girl's face and across her chest. She was bleeding from her nose and eyes, but he had no time to help her right then. He set her gently on the road.

"Hurry!" Fleeter said. Jack glanced back and saw the silvery trace of the bullet. It was already halfway between the sniper's rifle and its intended target, and Fleeter was standing at Reaper's side. "Remember, gentle," she said. "Just ease them aside. It'll hurt, but if you shove them over into the ground, the impact might kill them."

"Did it kill those guards?" he asked, but Fleeter did not answer. She was guiding Reaper to one side, lovingly, reverently, and Jack had to look away. That was his father she worshipped. A man he loved, and now the most brutal person he knew.

No, not quite. That title now went to Miller.

He stood in front of Sparky and Jenna and turned to watch the bullet, tracking its path. "It's him," Jack said. "Fleeter, it's my dad."

"Safe now," she said. "Kneel by the girl, flip back, make sure they see her."

"You think we can stop this now the first shot's been fired?"

She looked around more urgently. "Can't see any more flashes. Come on. Flip."

With a smack against the dulled air, Fleeter grew dull and motionless in Jack's vision.

He closed his eyes and did the same.

The gunshot and ricochet were deafening.

Jack gasped in a heavy breath, winded, and scooped the girl from the ground.

"Bloody hell!" Sparky said. "Where did you—?"

"We've got the girl!" Jack shouted. "And your torture doctors are dead! One more shot and the rest of you die too. Every . . . single . . . *one* of you!"

"Hold fire!" a voice shouted. It was electronically amplified, and Jack recognised Miller right away.

The rush of sound and input shocked Jack. The breeze against his face, his friends' heavy breathing, the rustle of clothing, mysterious, distant noises from elsewhere in the huge container park or beyond . . . he heard none of these when he was flipped. *I accelerate*, he thought, but knew that was not quite right. He could not fully explain what he and Fleeter could do.

The girl moved in his arms. She moaned something, and whined, and blood was still flowing from her nose and eyes. She was much too light, and he could feel bones he should not be able to feel. In using her, they had also neglected her. It was so brutal that it made him want to cry, or rage.

He chose rage.

"One more gunshot, you bastards, and you'll only kill one of us!" he shouted, voice echoing from stacked containers around the clearing. "That'll leave the rest, and others you can't see. Check on your torture hole. *Check* it!"

A rustle through the hidden loudspeaker, and then two Choppers jogged from different directions towards the doorway Jack and Fleeter had exited moments before. But they did not need to check. As they approached, a woman crawled into sight in the open doorway. She was on her hands and knees, bloodied head nodding slowly up and down, hair matted with gore. A high, soft keening came from her mouth, but Jack could not pity her.

"We'll kill them," Miller said. Faceless, voice crackling and distorted through speakers, he was more inhuman than ever. "The ones you want are still alive, but we'll kill them the moment something happens. One of you moves, one of you even *blinks*, and they die."

"We can be on you in less than a blink, Miller," Reaper said. His voice was low and casual, but it echoed from metal walls, and grit vibrated across the ground. Jack could already hear the fury in his father's voice. *Good*, he thought, elated. *Good! He* is *here to help. He* does *want Mum and Emily*.

The girl in Jack's arms opened her eyes. "Jamie?" she said.

"No, I'm not Jamie. My name's Jack."

The girl blinked bloodily, slowly raised a weak hand and wiped at her eyes. She looked at Jack for a few seconds, so sad, so soulful. His heart sank. He could have fallen in love with those eyes in an instant. "Oh," she said. "You're not Jamie."

He set her down, but kept an arm around her shoulder. Leaning against him for support, she felt dreadfully cold and weak.

"Every one of you," Jack said. "Every one of you, Miller! You'll be shooting at shadows, strangled by hands you can't see, seeing things you can't imagine. You think you know what the Irregulars can do, just because you've sliced them up and taken *samples* of their *brains*? You think you have even an inkling of what the Superiors can do, because you lose Choppers to them every week? Do you . . . do you have any idea what *I* can do?" He felt the others watching him—his friends, in fear; the Irregulars, nervous and yet ready to fight. And his father, with what might have been respect.

The scene fell almost silent. Hidden speakers crackled with Miller's doubt. Choppers stood tensed, uncertain, glancing down at their dropped weapons. Jack, Reaper, and the others faced them. And the girl leaned against Jack, starting to shiver with the knowledge that she had been released.

"We're the New," Jack said, loud enough for everyone to hear. "The fighting stops now. The killing ends here. You, Miller . . . you're the old. History. The past. And you know how the saying goes."

Beside him, Sparky chuckled softly then shouted, "Out with the old!"

"And in with the new," Jenna said.

"You really think we'd stay in London, here, without protection?" Miller said. "Without an insurance policy?" Jack was sure he could detect a note of resignation in the Chopper's voice.

"No good when you're dead," Reaper shouted.

"No more killing unless we have to, Dad," Jack said. Reaper did not even glance at his son as he started forward.

Puppeteer moved Choppers aside. Others backed away of their own accord, leaving their weapons where they had fallen. Jack and his friends followed, Breezer with them, and the New moved across Camp H unopposed.

Yet Jack felt no sense of victory. Something was wrong. The girl by his side was a living expression of Miller's inhumanity, and those rooms he had seen in the container buildings, the jars, the smears of blood and chunks of something—of *someone*—being cleared away . . .

With all that, could he ever really hope for peace?

As they approached the three joined containers, a door creaked open at the top of a gentle wooden ramp. Miller appeared strapped into a wheelchair, his terribly mutilated legs resting on footplates, his left arm ending in a stump just above his elbow. He looked thin and drawn, corpselike and lessened. Yet it was his smile that shocked Jack the most.

"Like your new chair, Miller," Reaper said. "Maybe this time I'll take your other arm, and your cock, and one of your eyes. Then how will you—"

Miller started laughing. He tilted his head back and guffawed at the sky, and Sparky and Jenna shot Jack a glance that said everything he was already thinking.

Something terrible was about to happen.

CHAPTER FIFTEEN
THE HOLLOW GIRL

"We need to leave," Rook said. "Really. Now. We're going the wrong way, Lucy-Anne!"

"Leave if you want, I'm going the *right* way."

They had been following Nomad since she had left. At least, Lucy-Anne had been leading them north. And soon after the strange woman had seemingly abandoned them, things had started to change. The wilderness around them had grown wilder, and more shapes and shadows made themselves known. They darted across hillsides and huddled beside lush growths of shrubs, and though the two of them kept to the open spaces, Lucy-Anne feared that soon they would meet more residents of the Heath.

Dusk approached, crawling across the hillsides like a living thing and driving the sun into the western expanses of London. Rook's birds drifted along above them like echoes of night, turning and spiralling up into the sky before swooping down again. Lucy-Anne was becoming used to their constant flap and swoosh, and she feared not hearing that anymore. *He's scared, he's terrified, and if he leaves me I'll be just as scared.*

Something burst from the trees ahead of them and came rapidly down the slope. Rook grasped her shoulder and pulled himself in front of her, squatted down, ready for a fight. He sent his birds and they angled in towards the shape, but then veered away at the last moment. Their *caw-caw*s sounded panicked to Lucy-Anne, and she dreaded meeting what could scare them so much.

But it was Nomad, only Nomad, and she grew from shadows to meet them.

Lucy-Anne went to her knees. *I've found him*, Nomad had said, and if that were the case, where was Andrew now?

"I'm . . . sorry," Nomad said. It was the most emotion Lucy-Anne had heard in her voice.

She took the gold chain and signet ring from Nomad's hand. Their parents had bought Andrew the ring for his eighteenth birthday, and the chain had been a present from one of his first girl-friends. His parting with her had been difficult, yet for some reason he'd still worn that chain, and treasured it. She'd once asked him why, and he'd told her it was because it reminded him of good times, not bad. She loved that about him—his positivity, and optimism.

"Where . . . ?" she asked.

"It doesn't matter," Nomad said. "You don't want to see."

I'll sleep, she thought. *I'll fall asleep and dream him alive and fine and laughing, and when I wake up . . .*

Lucy-Anne could not find her tears. She realised that she had not even cried for her parents, because from the moment their deaths had been confirmed to her everything had been Andrew, Andrew, all Andrew. And now . . .

"I've got nothing left," she said. She felt Rook's hand on her shoulder and remembered his dead brother, but it was Nomad she looked at. "Nothing. Nothing left at all. And . . . and you killed him. You killed my parents, and my brother."

Nomad's expression barely changed, but she did not look away.

Lucy-Anne knew she should be feeling rage at Nomad, and the Choppers, and everything that had happened to steal away her family. She should be grieving for her brother, who she had hoped would still be alive so that she was not now alone in this cruel new world. But she felt only a peculiar emptiness. Everything was distant to her, and she was a hollow girl.

"We need to get away from the Heath," Rook said. "Night's falling, and it feels strange. Like something terrible's about to happen."

"Something already is," Nomad said. And she told them.

Running again, always running, and Lucy-Anne so wished she could simply sit somewhere and fill her emptiness with grief.

But she feared that if she did, the grief would consume her. At least running, she had something else to think about. Rook held her hand and she so loved the contact, feeling a rush of affection for him as he squeezed her hand. They had both lost and found someone.

And she refused, totally, to lose anyone else.

On the back of the news about Andrew, Nomad's talk of the fate hanging over London had felt vaguely flat, almost uninteresting. But then Lucy-Anne had thought of Jack and Sparky, Jenna and Emily, and her heart had started sprinting in her chest. No. Not them as well. They were her friends—they had been her family for every second she had been on her own since Doomsday—and she would not let them die.

Running, always running, it took some time to even consider the possibility of her own death. It meant nothing.

Nomad had vanished again, and Lucy-Anne had let her go without a second glance. She could inspire no hatred for the strange woman or anger for what she had done. Perhaps over time, as her hollowness faded, that would come.

"It's not fair," Rook said, running with her. Birds swirled around them and took turns landing on his shoulders, and he kept tilting his head to hear their calls. They were scouting the way ahead and keeping a watch on their rear. He was doing his best to get them off Hampstead Heath safely, but with every step she sensed danger increasing. There was nothing specific—no shapes darting at them, no cries of attack—but a sense of doom had dropped over her that had nothing to do with Andrew.

It was the future that terrified her, and with every step they were closer to it.

"I guess maybe I knew he was dead," Lucy-Anne said.

"Not that," Rook said. "London. Everything they've done to it, what they've made it. And now . . ." He sounded like a child, and she could not feel angry at him. He didn't mean to lessen the impact of her brother's death. He had found a place for himself in London, and now everything was about to change again. What of Rook then? What of any of them?

"We'll get out," she said. "Find my friends, and all of us will get out."

"But what about my birds?"

You can set them free, she went to say, but realised that they were an integral part of him. Everyone left in London—Irregulars, Superiors, and anyone in between—belonged there now, and nowhere else.

"Maybe we can stop them," she said. Rook did not reply. Even if Nomad had stayed with them, it was a foolish idea.

"All these streets," Rook said. "All this city." He tilted his head as another rook landed on his shoulder, smiling as he glanced across at Lucy-Anne. "We're close. Just down this slope and through those trees, and we'll be—"

He vanished. Lucy-Anne ran on for a couple of seconds, barely registering what had happened. Her feet stamped through long grass, breeze ruffled through her dirty hair, her jacket flapped at her hips like loose wings. Pain kicked in across the back of her hand where Rook's nails had raked her skin, and as the gashes welled blood she heard his voice.

"Lucy-Anne!"

And then his scream.

She skidded to a stop, turned back and saw the hole in the ground, the stark edges of snapped branches protruding from where they had been laid across the pit. She could not see Rook, but his birds swooped around the pit and spiralled up again, taking up his cry, amplifying and echoing it, and she couldn't tell which was more bloodcurdling. She screamed herself, but did not hear. She smelled blackberries.

Please, no one else! she thought, because she had already lost too much. She went back to the hole and looked down. She wished the sun had set a little more.

Rook's scream faded as she saw what had happened to him, and with his one remaining eye he looked up at her. She hoped he saw her, but thought he was probably dead already, because the long, pale worm-thing—with its remnant of human limbs and filthy, tangled auburn hair—was pushing its snout deep into the hole it had torn in his throat and up beneath his unhinged jaw. It shook and scrabbled at the ground as it struggled to push its mouth deeper, and Lucy-Anne could smell the stench of freshly spilled blood.

"But I saved you," she said. "I saved you, I saved you, I—"

A rook tangled on her hair and pecked at her cheek. She swatted it away, then had to squeeze her eyes closed as two more came for her face. She punched at one and clawed at the other, and their cries as they swung away from her were heartrending. Loss rang out across that hillside. Lucy-Anne tripped and fell onto her back in the long grass, and looking up she saw the rooks circling higher and higher, an aerial dance for their dead master.

She crawled to the hole again and looked down, and the worm-thing was eating him now, chewing into his head with awful jaws. A crunching sound, a twitch of his body, and what remained of his face shifted sideways.

Unable to scream, not knowing what to say or do or think, she stood and ran down towards the trees, aimless and thoughtless, until she tripped over something hidden in the grass and smacked her head on the ground.

Vision faded, and sound grew distant. *I don't want to wake up*, Lucy-Anne thought as she drifted away. *Let me stay down here.*

Nomad is running towards her. She is in a burning street somewhere in London—buildings are aflame, a vehicle has exploded, bodies litter the road and pavements, and someone is staggering across the road, crying wretchedly as they try to gather their unspooling guts.

Lucy-Anne holds up her hands, but she cannot speak. She tries to back away from Nomad, but her feet will not obey her. She can do nothing as the woman runs closer, jumping past a burning motorcycle whose flames barely seem to touch her.

In the distance, gunfire. Closer by, the sound of heavy footsteps. Bullets strike the road and kick up gravel and dust.

Everything seems to be converging on her.

Nomad reaches her and does not stop running. She knocks Lucy-Anne to the ground and sits astride her, raising one hand high above her head with two fingers pointing down, like a child forming its hand into a gun.

This is my dream, Lucy-Anne thinks, *and whatever happens next I can just dream away.*

Nomad's hand strikes down and her stiff fingers punch a hole directly into Lucy-Anne's throat.

But this is my . . .

CHAPTER SIXTEEN
BIG BINDY

Jack had been wrong. A terrible thing was not about to happen. He thought perhaps it already had.

"He's laughing even though he's lost," Jack said.

"Guy looks seriously screwed," Sparky said. "Your old man do that to him, mate?"

Jack caught Reaper's eye. Reaper looked as hard and determined as ever, but a shadow of doubt shaded his eyes. He was not quite as in control of this situation as he'd hoped.

"The first move they make, kill them," Reaper said, and he started forward.

"Jenna!" Jack said urgently. His friend nodded because she knew exactly what he wanted—she came to him and took the girl, hugging her close even though she stank. Jack saw the sympathy in his friend's eyes and loved her even more.

Jack started forward and Sparky came with him. Behind them were Breezer and the Irregulars. Fleeter walked close with Reaper, exaggerating the swing of her hips and enjoying the moment, even after what they had just seen and done. As they approached the first of the terrified soldiers she flipped, and the air boomed as it filled the space she had occupied. The Choppers glanced around in a panic. She could have been readying to gut any one of them.

From up on the container stacks, four soldiers were lowered roughly to the ground, their twisted and broken weapons dropping with them. One of them cried out as he struck the ground, and Jack heard the sickening sound of breaking bone. *Puppeteer*, he thought.

At least he hadn't killed them. He caught movement from the corner of his eye and knew that Shade was there also, and perhaps a couple of other Superiors he had yet to meet.

This felt very much like the final confrontation, and though they were all there and Miller was exposed, Jack was certain that somehow they no longer had the advantage.

Reaper turned to Jack and Breezer and said, "You two and me. Seems appropriate." He walked towards Miller, and Jack and Breezer went with him. They were representatives of their alliance— Irregular, Superior, and Jack from outside. As they closed on Miller, Jack knew he had to speak first.

"The New are united against you and everything you've done. And you've lost, Miller."

In the doorway before them, Miller laughed again. This close he was grotesque, only part of a man. Yet his laughter was heartfelt, and Jack thought perhaps he wasn't yet mad.

"*You've* lost, Jack," he said. "All of you were lost, from the moment Doomsday ended and we took control of London. We've been letting your father and his cronies have their fun since then, but your end was inevitable. You just didn't know it."

"Shut up," Reaper said. "Shade?" Shade appeared behind Miller and pressed a knife across his throat. Miller tensed and grew quiet, but the laughter did not leave his eyes.

Jack should have waited. There might have been guards hiding in there with machine guns at the ready, or traps designed to gut the unwary. But he could not wait, not after all this time. He grabbed Miller's wheelchair and used it to haul himself up into the container, pushed past Shade, and entered the shadowy interior.

After seeing inside the other place he'd expected something high-tech. What he saw was the exact opposite. Inside the first container was a rough seating area, with chairs around the edges, a few camping tables scattered with polystyrene cups and food wrappers, and a gun rack on one wall. At the far end were several camp beds, with a curtained area that might have been a toilet. The floor was messed with sawdust and lined with tracks from Miller's wheelchair.

Two Choppers stood facing Jack, guns in their hands. He reached for the pistol in his belt and drew it slowly, keeping a careful watch on their faces, eyes, hands. But they looked terrified. *If they move I'll just flip*, he thought, *or shout, or I'll melt their gun barrels before they can even shoot.*

As the pistol left his belt, the two Choppers dropped their guns and edged around him towards the door.

"Get out," Jack said. They scampered away, and he watched Shade kick them out past Miller's wheelchair.

A heavy curtain hid a doorway into the middle container. He grabbed it and pulled it aside, hooks squealing on the metal curtain pole to reveal a poorly lit area with heavy cages stacked on either side. They resembled large dog crates, and were fixed in place by roughly welded metal bars.

The cages held people.

"Mum!" Jack called. "Emily!"

There was movement in the shadows as the prisoners stirred, trying to stretch limbs against their confinement. The place stank of human waste, unwashed bodies, gone-off food. Hopelessness. Jack's eyes watered from the smell, and from tears of rage.

"Emily! Mum!"

"Jack," a weak, quiet voice said, and Jack's heart broke. His little sister, Emily, locked away like an animal, filthy, weak, terrified, and hopeless, he dashed to her cage and knelt so that they could touch each other's fingers through the grille.

"Oh, Emily," he said through his tears.

"Son?"

"Mum!" He looked behind him at one of the cages stacked higher, and his mother was there. She looked strong, and proud. "I came for you," he said. "*All* of you." Everyone was stirring now, and he guessed there were a dozen people locked away in there. He didn't understand how they could exist in such conditions, but he was here to set them free, now. And on the way out, he would see Miller.

He gripped the gun tighter in his hand. Then he shoved it in his belt and tried to rationalise his anger. Murder was not in his nature.

"Rosemary?" he asked. His mother's head dipped, and that was all the answer he needed.

"Jack," Emily said, her voice breaking. He knelt by her again and they entwined fingers through the thick wires. Her tears cleared streaks down her face, and Jack blinked away his own. His little sister was so strong and resourceful, and since Doomsday she had looked after him as much as the other way around. He loved her more than anything or anyone, and he was shaking at how close he had come to losing her.

"Come on," he said. "I'll get you out, then we're leaving. All of us."

"And we'll get my camera on the way?" she asked.

"Oh, Emily." He couldn't believe how brave she was being. But as he stood and readied to release the pathetic prisoners, he thought that the camera might be a very good idea. Things were changing rapidly inside London, but that didn't mean that anything was different on the outside. They would still need proof to expose the truth.

"Everybody back from your cage doors," he said.

"Jack, what are you doing?" his mother asked.

"Lots has happened, Mum. Dad's outside."

"Oh," she breathed. He hated that she sounded so vulnerable.

There was a rustle of clothing and a few tired groans as they shuffled back in their small cages—too small to stand in or lie out straight—and then Jack breathed deeply and closed his eyes. He tasted Nomad's finger, the tang of everything she had given him, and then he zeroed in on a gleaming point in his mind.

"Hurry," a voice said behind him. It sounded like Fleeter. He hated the idea that she had been watching him all along, and he had not heard the impact of her manifesting behind him. But he knew she was right. There was a balance of power here, and it would only take one Chopper to pick up a gun for chaos to descend.

Then there would be rapid, terrible slaughter.

Jack grunted, and three padlocks crunched apart. He turned slightly and focussed again, sending the concentrated power elsewhere. Four more times, and then he kicked at the bars and sent broken metal tinkling to the floor.

Fleeter helped. She threw cage doors open and looked inside, moving on to the next, and the next. Jack realised that she was searching for someone.

Emily stood and gripped hold of him. She buried her face in his shirt and cried, and then he felt his mother's arms about both of them. He closed his eyes and lost himself in her feel and her smell, and for the briefest moment he was eight again and they were back at home, happy.

"Damn it!" Fleeter said. Jack opened his eyes. She was shoving past people standing uncertainly, finding their feet after incarceration in these tiny cages. One man cried out and slipped to the floor, but Fleeter did not apologise or help him up.

"We've got them," Jack said. "Come on." But he already knew that this was something else.

"You go," Fleeter said.

"There," Jack's mother said. "They're through there, in the next one. They torture them often."

Jack looked down into his sister's haunted face, and then the other prisoners, all of them staring towards the dark opening into the next container.

"You go," Fleeter said again to Jack.

"What's back there?"

She came close to him, and she was more human than he had ever seen her. She reached out and touched his cheek. "Take your family, sweetheart," she said. "Get out. Run. This is all going to go bad."

"No," Jack said. "No, this is the changing point. This is when peace begins."

"Peace?" Fleeter asked. Her grin returned. "Who wants peace? This is too much fun." She pulled a pocket torch and went through into the next container. Jack saw the heavier bars of larger cages beyond, and then Fleeter was fiddling with padlocks and locks.

"Son," his mother said. "There's nothing good back there. You're a brave, good boy. Lead us out."

"But I can do things, Mum," he said. "Amazing things."

"So I see. Then amaze us all away from here. This place is evil."

Jack led them out. Miller had been moved down the ramp now, and Reaper stood behind his wheelchair, looking for all the world like someone taking a sick friend for a walk. His hands rested on the chair's handles. Miller looked scared, but defiant.

"Where are they?" Reaper asked.

"Here," Jack said. He jumped down and lifted Emily down to the ground, then held out his hand for his mother.

"Daddy!" Emily said. Their mother did not speak, because she already knew the truth.

"Where are they?" Reaper asked again. He had barely glanced at his family, and as the other freed prisoners started climbing down, wincing against the dusky light, he virtually ignored them all.

"Fleeter's getting them," he said. "Mum said there are two left."

"Only two," Reaper said. He looked down at the wasted man before him, and Jack thought he was going to destroy Miller there and then.

But Miller was a man for whom survival had become an art.

"You're all going to die," he said. He looked at Jack, then down at Emily. "Every single one of you."

"And you'll be the first," Jack said. He drew the pistol. It seemed fitting, somehow, to kill this murdering bastard with a bullet instead of a special power.

"Er, Jack?" Sparky said. He was standing to one side, and Emily dashed to him and hugged him, seeking refuge.

"Jack," Reaper said. "This one doesn't die."

"Won't killing him be the victory you want?" Jack asked. He pointed the gun at Miller's face. The man's smile barely wavered.

"Kill? If you think that means anything anymore, you really don't understand what London has become. No, like I said . . . this one doesn't die." Reaper rested a hand on Miller's shoulder, and the mutilated man's smile fell at last. "I get to play with him some more."

"What do you mean?" Jack asked Miller. "What's happening? What have you done?"

"Fail-safe," Miller said. "Big Bindy." He laughed again. "I named it myself. Bindy was my wife, and she was big, and she was . . . destructive."

"Tell us," Reaper said.

"Who's Big Bindy?" Scryer asked.

"She's a bomb designed to destroy what's left of London," Miller said, frowning as he gushed the truth. "A nuclear bomb. Buried. Fifteen megatons."

"Where?" Scryer asked.

"I don't know," he said. "They don't let anyone into London who knows. I'm just . . ."

"Expendable," Reaper said. "Like all of us."

"None of you are expendable," Miller said. "You're already

spent. Dead people walking. You're memories, and no one outside will miss you when you die, because you're already dead."

"You'll die too," Jack said. "If they blow the bomb, you'll all die."

"It doesn't matter anymore," Miller said. "I've just pushed the button. Tick-tock, Jack. Tick-tock, tick-tock . . ."

"Reaper!" Fleeter called from the doorway, excited. "They're drugged and tied." She look at Jack, surprised that he was still there.

Puppeteer climbed up next to her and entered the darkness, and moments later two people floated out through the doorway, lowering gently to the ground. A man and a woman, they were bound in heavy chains, limbs tied behind them, gagged, and their skin was pale and slick. They both looked dead, but Jack knew better.

"Who are they?" Jack asked.

"Friends," Reaper said. He knelt beside the prone woman and touched her face, and one of her eyelids flickered open. Her eye was a startling blue, and her breath misted the air.

"And what can *they* do?"

Reaper ignored him. "The others?" he asked Fleeter.

It was Miller who answered. "We cut them up. Dissected their brains. Threw their remains out for the wild dogs."

Reaper tensed, his face thunderous. "You should leave," he said to Jack. "All of you."

"Dad—"

"This is no place for you."

"Daddy?" Emily said.

"This is no place for you!" Reaper's voice did not rise in volume, but the side of the container behind them caved in, metal shrieking, rending.

"No," Jack said. "Not like this. We've got a chance, here."

"Against him and his like?" Reaper asked, nudging Miller.

"Peace is the only answer," Jack said. "If we leave now, and you kill everyone here, what do you think happens next?"

"Big Bindy," Reaper said. "But we'll find it and disable it. They'd have left themselves time to get all the Choppers out of London. We'll have a day, maybe more."

"And if you can't disable it?"

"We will," Reaper said. "London is ours. Our playground, and our home. It'll always be ours from now on, and him and his like . . . amusing distractions."

"Distractions that will catch you and cut you up," Jack said. "Like they did to Rosemary. And so many others. And they released the sickness, Dad. Are you sure it won't touch you? Your Superiors? Allow peace, and maybe they'll release the cure."

"I've released nothing," Miller said.

"But they're dying," Jack said.

"So will you, boy. And everyone who uses their unnatural, unholy powers too much. Your brains can't handle it. Evolve is *imperfect*. The more you use your talents, the closer you take yourselves to death."

"How can you know that?"

Miller smiled but did not reply.

"Because he's looked at a lot of brains," Sparky said.

"And because he *created* Evolve!" Breezer said, amazed, and yet with a certainty assured by his own talent. "It was *him!* Angelina Walker released it, but it was always Miller's baby."

"And they'd never let me test it. Not on humans, at least. Can't blame them." He chuckled. "Dear Angelina and I talked about releasing it, but I never believed she'd go through with it. I wouldn't have. But then she did, and . . ." He smiled, because they knew the rest of the story.

"And London became your own ready-made lab," Jack said.

"Finish him, Reaper," Fleeter said.

"No." Reaper looked up, and Jack saw the fire in his eyes. "I've only just begun with him."

This was my greatest hope, Jack thought. *And now it's going to explode*. His mother and sister were with him, but his father had become a monster. The future hinged on this moment, and yet even though he had helped bring things this way, Jack realised he had never had any control. This was all Miller and Reaper, and the awful game they played—Miller experimenting; Reaper revelling.

"Let us go first, Dad," Jack said, and in one last attempt, one final plea, he forced a memory into his father's head.

The four of them walk around a castle in North Wales. Emily is a toddler, singing her own song as she explored the nooks and crannies. Jack is not quite a teenager, and he's taking rubbings from some of the stone detail. His mother and father are holding hands. Jack has caught them kissing at least twice today, and he looks back frequently. They look so happy. It's starting to rain.

"Don't . . . do . . . that," Reaper said, and all across the camp people shivered. *That's it*, Jack thought. *That's all I can do*.

"Mum," Jack said, turning around. "We have to leave."

His mother was looking at Reaper, and for a moment Jack saw a flash of love from his memory. But reality had hardened his mother. Whatever his naive hopes had been, she had always known the truth.

"Go with them," he heard Reaper say. He glanced back, and Puppeteer and Fleeter were looking at Jack, waiting for him to leave. He was surprised, but he didn't express it. He didn't even thank his father.

They trooped from Camp H, collecting Jenna and the weak girl on the way. Sparky helped Jenna support the girl between them. Jack and Emily held hands. His mother and some of the released prisoners followed, and Breezer and his Irregulars followed on behind. Puppeteer hurried on ahead, seemingly keen to not walk with them, and Fleeter flipped out with a *crack!*

"So the New ends here," Jack said to Breezer walking close by.

"Don't think it ever really began," Breezer said. "Like I told you when we first met, your father's a monster."

"The bomb?" Jack asked.

Breezer shook his head. "First I've heard of it. But he was speaking the truth."

"So we have to get out," Jack said. "All of us."

"Reaper was right. There'll be time. I'll gather as many Irregulars as I can, but . . ."

"But they'll only let out the Choppers."

"And the way we came in is known to them now," Jack's mother said. "That's where they caught us. Us, and poor Rosemary. She fought so hard."

"She saved my life," Jenna said sadly.

"I can get us through," Jack said.

Behind them, someone screamed.

"Let's go!" Sparky said. They all started to run, but Jack could not flee without seeing. He had to know. Had to see what games his father and Miller were really playing, and why such potential that the New had presented must be squandered. He stopped at the entrance to the route back through the storage park and turned to watch.

Using our talents kills us in the end, Jack thought. Miller could have very good reasons to lie about that—to make them all afraid of using their talents. But there was also a good chance it was true.

The bomb. The sickness. The end of Camp H. Everything was drawing to a close, and the only way he could salvage anything from the tragedy of Doomsday was to make the end a new beginning.

He watched as Shade and the others forced the Choppers together into a group before the larger of the two container units.

The soldiers were plainly terrified, but the Superiors were unconcerned. They were smiling. Enjoying this.

Reaper moved from behind Miller and knelt again by the bound
woman's side. He sat her up and allowed her to lean back against
him, whispering to her, smiling when she nodded, stroking her
matted hair. Puppeteer grimaced with concentration as he used his
power to bend and break chains, and twist ropes until they frayed
and snapped. In his chair, Miller looked like a shrunken old man
now, head bowed, all the bluster gone from him. It was he who had
screamed—blood coated the side of his head, and Jack thought perhaps his father had torn off an ear.

He's no longer my father. For the first time, Jack really meant that.
His heart beat in fear at what he was about to see. He could close his
eyes. He could leave. But everything he had been through already
meant that it was important to bear witness.

Jack glanced back at the others—strangers, and people he loved.
He raised a hand with two fingers up: two minutes. But he didn't
think it would take that long.

The Superiors backed away from the group of twenty or more
Choppers. Still propped against Reaper's side, the woman raised her
newly released hands and pointed. The air around her head misted as
she breathed out. The chains still gathered around her legs glimmered with frost.

One of the Choppers screamed, because she knew what was
going to happen. And when she ran, she did not get far.

Even from where he watched, Jack felt the gush of cold air. It
tickled his nose and burned his skin, and the woman who'd tried to
run ground to a slow, painful halt. It was like watching a film of
someone slowed down, and then . . . Freeze-frame.

Reaper smiled, then whispered, and the power of his voice shattered the frozen woman.

Other Choppers ran. The woman shouted. The luckiest made twenty paces before their flesh started to freeze, muscles cramping and then tearing at the sudden, impossible temperature change, blood coagulating, and every scrap of agony was visible on their stilled expressions. Several of them fell and broke apart as they struck the ground, and Jack could not help wondering whether they remained conscious of what was happening to them, just for a moment.

In his chair, Miller sat with Shade grasping his head. He'd been made to watch every moment.

Mass murder complete, Reaper looked across at Jack. He smiled. He'd known all along that his son was watching.

Then Reaper let the woman gently lie down and turned to Miller, and as Jack ran for his friends and family, he heard the wretched man screaming again, and his father's laughter.

For the first time in two years, Nomad was as close to a normal woman as she could be.

He's doing his best for the people he loves. He's brave. But Jack will soon realise that his responsibilities have expanded. His is a wider outlook now, and he'll only see that when he stops seeking inward for all those new potentials. That part will soon become as natural as breathing. For me that universe is a wild, violent place filled with chaos and uncertainty . . . difficult for me to grasp . . . too filled with pain.

But for Jack it will be beautiful.

She took in a deep breath and felt the pain in her chest, so real and *there* that it surprised her again with each inhalation. Even stretching her senses out to Jack was starting to hurt. She had reined in everything else she was so used to doing, because it was all starting to pain her more—knowing London through movement and scent, avoiding detection when she so desired, sitting motionless in the river of time while moments passed her by. She concentrated on Jack and one other, because the future of London was with them both.

This is his greatest challenge yet. It will be the making of him, or his undoing. And her purity can only help. The bomb is hidden away so well that . . . even I . . .

Nomad sought again, but she felt a warm trickle across her lips and tasted blood. The world swam. She floated in it, and now and then was aware of glances from those few she passed by—deeply knowledgeable from those she had once thought of as monsters; confused, scared, from the rest of London's people.

They see change in me and that frightens them. And so it should.

It certainly frightened Nomad.

Miller. Did you know? Were you aware that Evolve was far from perfect?

The potential for perfection lay in Jack. And in Lucy-Anne, suffering from another dreadful blow and yet still the one who might save them all. Pure and untainted by Evolve, her own unique talent was already growing larger, and larger.

If Jack and Lucy-Anne failed, or let their true aims die beneath human concerns, then London would be finished.

And I will willingly let it go.

Whether Nomad would go with it, or persist like the spirit-man she had met in the north, there was only one way to know.

"I can't leave," Jack said. Night had fallen. They were close to the bombed wastelands of London's borders now, ready to go down and through the network of tunnels and sewers to the outside. The Irregulars they had rescued had drifted away, back into the ruined city they now called home. Breezer and his people had gone to spread the word about Big Bindy, and Puppeteer had vanished without warning several hours before. Fleeter remained, but at a distance.

With everything that had happened to him, Jack was suddenly scared at the normality beyond London's borders.

"I never thought you would," his mother said.

"Gotta find Lucy-Anne," Jenna said.

"Yeah." Sparky chuckled. "And, you know, we've had such a lot of fun here, why *would* we leave?"

"Idiot." Jenna poked him in the ribs, and it turned into a hug.

"You'll make sure they get through safely," he said to Fleeter. She nodded, eyes glittering. "Then I'll be back."

"Of course. Lots more Choppers to kill." Jack's sarcasm was heavy, but he knew it was the truth. He understood that, now. The Superiors saw this as a game, and the Irregulars and Choppers were their pawns.

But London's future was now shrinking with every second that passed, and Jack had no idea what that might mean for everyone still here.

"We're not going either, Jack," Jenna said.

"Jenna—" Jack began, but Sparky grabbed him in a neck-lock. Jenna stepped forward and dragged her knuckles back and forth across his scalp, and Jack snorted in pain and pleasure. They were playing.

"Well, now, you gonna use your special powers to *make* me go?" Sparky asked.

"I could," Jack wheezed.

"Yeah. I don't doubt that." Sparky let him go, and Jack rubbed his neck as he looked around at them all.

"You're special, too," Jack said to Sparky and Jenna. "Both of you. It's both of you who've stopped me going mad with all this. You're my . . . reality."

They were all silent for a moment, and then Sparky said, "Pussy."

Jack grinned, then turned to his sister. "Emily, you need to retrieve that camera you hid before you were caught. Start spreading the news. Mum, don't go home. Cornwall, West Wales, somewhere like that. Be careful whom you tell and how, but start getting those pictures out onto the net. Emily is . . . well, you'd be surprised at how good she's become at computer stuff."

"I'm not at all surprised," his mother said, smiling lovingly at her daughter. She was thinner than she'd ever been, face drawn, and she'd aged ten years in two. But she was filled with love for her children, and that made her glow.

"What about me?" the girl said. She'd recovered her strength quickly as the drugs had started working from her system. Her name was Rhali.

"You're welcome to come with us," Emily said.

Rhali looked back and forth between them, but her eyes always settled on Jack.

"I think perhaps I'll stay with you," she said. Jack nodded. He would take any help he could get.

"Jack—" his mother began.

"Mum, I'll be careful," he said.

"I wasn't going to say that, son. I was going to tell you how proud I am."

Jack pursed his lips and nodded, trying not to cry. There had been too many tears. They all hugged silently, and then it was time.

He, Rhali, Jenna, and Sparky watched Fleeter leading Emily and his mother through the darkness and underground. Jack felt an awful tug watching them go. He had been desperate to find and rescue them, and now that he had he was letting them go again. But he also had every confidence that Fleeter would see them safely through and out of London. Outside, they had their own work to do. And in London, he had his.

"Right then," Sparky said, clapping his hands together. "Reaper's at war, Miller's pushed the button on a nuclear bomb that'll explode at any time and flatten London, any Choppers left are out to avenge their dead friends. And I'm bloody staving. So what's next?"

The four of started walking back the way they'd come, but no one answered Sparky's final question.

None of them could know.

ACKNOWLEDGMENTS

Thanks as always to my agent Howard Morhaim, and to my editor Lou Anders.

ABOUT THE AUTHOR

TIM LEBBON is a *New York Times*-bestselling writer from South Wales. He's had almost thirty novels published to date, as well as dozens of novellas and hundreds of short stories. His most recent releases include *Coldbrook* from Arrow/Hammer, *London Eye* (book one of the Toxic City trilogy) from Pyr in the United States, *Nothing as It Seems* from PS Publishing, and *The Heretic Land* from Orbit, as well as the Secret Journeys of Jack London series (coauthored with Christopher Golden), *Echo City*, and the *Cabin in the Woods* novelisation. Future novels include *Into the Void: Dawn of the Jedi (Star Wars)* from Del Rey/Star Wars Books. He has won four British Fantasy Awards, a Bram Stoker Award, and a Scribe Award, and has been a finalist for International Horror Guild, Shirley Jackson, and World Fantasy Awards.

Fox 2000 acquired film rights to *The Secret Journeys of Jack London*, and he and Golden wrote the first draft of the screenplay. A TV series of his Toxic City trilogy is in development with ABC Studios in the United States, and he's also working on new screenplays, both solo and in collaboration with Stephen Volk.

Find out more about Tim at his website, www.timlebbon.net.